THE MODEL MYSTERY

THE MODEL MYSTERY

REBECCA PRICE JANNEY

WORD PUBLISHING

Dallas·London·Vancouver·Melbourne

THE MODEL MYSTERY

Managing Editor : Laura Minchew
Project Editor: Beverly Phillips

Library of Congress Cataloging–in–Publication Data

Janney, Rebecca Price, 1957–
    The model mystery / Rebecca Price Janney.
        p.   cm.—(The Heather Reed mystery series ; #2) "Word kids!"
    Summary: Working as a substitute reporter for a teen magazine,
sixteen-year-old Heather Reed works to uncover who is behind the
threats to two top competitors in the American Model of the Year contest.
    ISBN 0–8499–3835–X
    [1. Mystery and detective stories.   2. Beauty contests—fiction.]
    I. Title.   II. Series : Janney, Rebecca Price, 1957–   Heather Reed
mystery series ; #2.
PZ7.J2433Mo   1993
[Fic]—dc20   92–45710

                                                                    CIP
                                                                    AC

Printed in the United States

3 4 5 6 7 8 9 LBM 9 8 7 6 5 4 3 2 1

My special thanks to Marsha Peltz of the Valley Forge Music Fair, Sergeant Bruce Penuel, the Collegeville (PA) Police Department, and Scott—a model husband.

Contents

Opportunity Knocks

"Dad!" Heather Reed jumped up from her seat in the auditorium and kissed her father on the cheek. Heather had been sitting with her brother Brian and his college roomate, Joe Rutli. "What brings you to the Philadelphia Music Fair?" the sixteen-year-old girl asked her father. She referred to the theater where the The American Model of the Year Contest was taking place.

"I just wanted to see how y'all are making out," Patrick Reed smiled broadly. Having lived in the North for twenty years, Mr. Reed still had not lost his Southern accent—or his love of bright clothes. Today he was wearing a bold plaid tie.

That one's not too bad, Heather grinned as she thought of some of the other neckties her dad owned. Mr. Reed shook hands with the boys and took a seat next to his daughter.

Suddenly Heather's best friend, sixteen-year-old Jenn McLaughlin, burst into the auditorium. Jenn's face shone with excitement. "I actually met Luke Granger and Marci

Bentley!" she gushed. "He looked like a Greek statue with his wavy hair and dreamy eyes. And that smile!" She sighed contentedly.

"Way to go, Jenn! Did you get the job?" asked Heather.

"Who are Luke and Marci?" Mr. Reed interrupted.

"They're models," Heather laughed.

Then Jenn breathlessly explained, "I got a job as their attendant. Imagine! I'll be working for Luke—and Marci—for the entire American Model of the Year Contest. Their wishes will be my commands."

"If you don't faint every time you look at Luke," Brian said under his breath.

"Do I detect some jealousy?" his father teased.

His son's face reddened. Jenn had had a crush on Brian Reed for years, but now it seemed the Kirby College freshman had some competition.

"Brian and Joe landed interesting jobs, too," Heather remarked.

"It was really cool, Mr. Reed." Joe's animated face looked even livelier than usual. "We were standing around, and this guy approached us."

"Steven Ramsey," Brian added. "The contest coordinator."

Joe nodded. "That's right. And he asked if we'd be escorts for the contestants."

"What a break!" Mr. Reed said.

"We're even getting paid for it!" Brian remarked.

His father laughed at this last comment and said, "Those models will be fighting to have you two as their escorts, I'm sure." Then he asked his daughter, "What will you be doing, Heather? I can't imagine your getting left out."

"Jenn thinks I should enter the contest." The way she said it made the very idea seem laughable.

"I don't know why not," Jenn scolded. "You're so pretty, and I would kill for a figure like that!"

Though Jenn was attractive in a spunky way with her short red hair and blue eyes, she had broad shoulders and hips. She had tried dieting, but nothing could change her large frame.

"I'm too short," Heather repeated. "Those contestants tower over me! Besides, they've been preparing for months. You don't just jump into something like that."

Mr. Reed cleared his throat. "So, Heather, how will you get involved in the contest?"

She smiled impishly. "I smell a mystery."

"It's trouble as usual," Brian complained. The eighteen-year-old had watched his sister get into scrapes ever since he could remember.

Heather lifted her chin. "There's something strange going on around here," she insisted. "I can feel it."

"And what is that?" Brian challenged.

"The tension here is as thick as the dust in your room," she stated.

"You imagine things," he scoffed.

"No, Brian, she doesn't," came a woman's voice.

All heads turned in Chloé St. Johns' direction. They usually did. Her dusky skin, amber eyes, and willowy figure captured attention. At one time Chloé was the highest-paid model in France. But after marrying an American businessman, she had moved to the United States. Now in her mid forties, Chloé St. Johns was the fashion editor of *The Philadelphia Journal,* Mr. Reed's paper.

"Chloé, I was hoping I'd run into you here," Patrick Reed said. "We need to discuss your coverage of the contest since you'll be one of the judges."

"Cetainly," she responded. "What brings all of you to the American Model of the Year Contest?"

"We've been watching the media photo sessions of the contestants," said Heather.

"Brian and Joe are going to be escorts, and I'm Luke Granger and Marci Bentley's assistant," Jenn added proudly.

"I still don't know if I've ever seen these models, Luke and Marci," Mr. Reed said.

"They're the highest-paid models in the country. They make thousands of dollars a day," Jenn said.

"And *you* switched to newspaper work?" Patrick Reed asked his fashion writer in disbelief.

"One does age," she laughed.

"You're still beautiful," Joe blurted out. Then he turned almost purple with embarrassment.

"Anyway," Jenn interrupted, "Marci and Luke also work for Pep Shampoo, which is sponsoring the contest."

"Of course!" Mr. Reed said. "I've seen the TV commercials. Isn't she the one with big hair?"

Everyone laughed.

"That's her all right," Chloé St. Johns said. Then she became serious. "Heather, do you have a job?"

"She's sniffing out another mystery," Brian laughed.

"Heather, don't let them give you a hard time," said the former model. "I, too, believe something is not right here. But you really picked it up quickly."

Just as Chloé began to say something else, a loud crash came from the stage area, followed by a chorus of air-splitting screams.

2

Deadly Threat

Stunned and screaming contestants scattered into the aisles of the theater-in-the-round auditorium. A cloud of dust rose from the stage and met the swinging lights above.

Heather saw that one of the enormous overhead lights had fallen and exploded against the stage.

She couldn't tell if anyone had been injured.

"Let's see if we can help!" Mr. Reed suggested. He and Heather led the way toward the stage where the media were reorganizing to record the accident. Contest coordinator Steven Ramsey was waving his arms frantically from the stage as the scene grew more chaotic.

"Please calm down everyone!" he commanded. "Will the reporters please give the girls some breathing room!"

Heather walked boldly onto the stage to examine the fallen light and instantly spotted the problem. *Someone cut this cable!*

"Hey! Get away from there!" Steven Ramsey ordered her to leave.

"Didn't get too far, huh?" Joe sympathized when she rejoined the others.

"Actually I did," she said. "The cable that holds the light in place was severed."

"Severed?" Jenn asked loudly.

"Shh!" Heather warned.

When they discovered no one had been harmed, Chloé asked the others to follow her outside.

"I have something important to tell you," Chloé said, knowing Heather's love of a good mystery. "The stage-light accident is not the only thing that upset the models today."

"What else happened?" Heather asked, wondering whether Chloé knew something about the tension she had sensed at the contest.

"At this morning's rehearsal one of the contestants fainted."

"What was wrong with her?" Jenn asked.

"I do not know," Chloé remarked. "I went immediately to her side while someone called an ambulance. She whispered very softly, 'I can't take this.'"

"Did they take her to the hospital?" asked Heather, shifting her leather backpack from one shoulder to the other.

"No. The paramedics revived her fully, and she got up on her own. I wanted very much to discover more," she said, "so I came back this afternoon to find out how she felt."

"Is she here?" Heather asked.

"Yes. A little while ago I asked how she felt," Chloé said. "Though she told me, 'Fine,' she was very pale."

"Maybe it's a case of nerves," Mr. Reed suggested. "She's probably under a lot of stress."

"Which one is she?" Heather questioned.

"Kirsten Neff. And yes, I do think she is sick with worry, but not because of winning or losing," she said. "I have a feeling her life may be in danger, especially since that stage light fell."

"How are the other contestants acting?" Brian asked.

"In fact I heard a group of them discussing Miss Neff behind her back. They seemed to think she was, uh, a wimp," Chloé said.

"So what do you make of the situation?" Heather pursued.

"I fear that Kirsten is in some kind of danger," she concluded. "Perhaps you can find out what it is, Heather? I understand you've got a reputation for solving mysteries."

Heather blushed. Sometimes she was embarrassed about all the attention the press had focused on her when she discovered information regarding an assassination attempt against the director of the C.I.A.

"I'll sure try." Then the teenager told Chloé about her own hunch.

"She can't just hang around," Brian objected.

"I really do need a cover," she agreed.

"That will not be difficult. That is, if your father does not protest," Chloé added quickly. "I can arrange for you to represent a teen magazine at the competition."

Jenn squealed. "That's wonderful! Which magazine?"

"*Star Struck*," the ex-model said.

Jenn was beside herself. "I read that all the time! It's so cool."

"It's really popular," she agreed. "May I, Dad?"

He shook his head and smiled. "Well, since it's spring break and it won't interfere with your school work, it's okay with me. But now I've got to get back to the office. I'll see you this evening."

"Thanks!" Heather said, hugging him.

The rest of the group went back to the auditorium.

Chloé explained that the magazine had assigned a reporter to the American Model of the Year Contest, but a family emergency had prevented her from coming.

The fashion editor quickly made the necessary arrangements with *Star Struck*'s editor, Rhonda Cowley, who was very pleased. Ms. Cowley talked to Heather on the phone and gave her some general instructions. Then she promised to fax Heather's press credentials immediately and to send a photographer the next day.

"I think I'll hang around here this afternoon and see what I can find out," Heather told the others when she returned from the phone.

Brian protested, "I don't want to spend the rest of the day inside. We'll be cooped up enough with our contest jobs."

Still trying to decide what to do for the rest of the afternoon, Brian, Jenn, and Joe told Heather they'd meet her at the Hot Spot restaurant next to the Music Fair at five-thirty.

When Heather returned to the main part of the theater with Chloé, she heard one contestant threaten to sue everyone in sight.

"Who's that?" she asked.

"Ashley Pitman. She and Kirsten Neff are considered the front runners."

"I wonder what she's so upset about."

Chloé laughed. "It could be anything. That girl is very demanding."

Another model heard the comment as she walked by. "A hair is probably out of place," she sneered.

The fashion editor excused herself to make phone calls, and Heather was on her own. Workers had begun repairing the damage to the stage lights, which delayed the afternoon rehearsal. Heather stood next to Steven Ramsey and his assistant Joan Winchell, hoping to pick up some clues.

"Have you seen Jean-Paul?" he asked Ms. Winchell.

She sighed. "He's all over the place."

"What a loose canon!" Ramsey said in disgust.

I wonder if they mean THE Jean-Paul? Heather thought. Jean-Paul was a famous designer. One of his blouses alone cost several hundred dollars.

"This is taking far too long," Steven Ramsey complained.

Heather decided to introduce herself.

The middle-aged man's eyes narrowed. "Didn't I meet you already?"

"Not really," she answered quickly, remembering how

he'd shooed her off the stage. "What can you tell me about the accident?"

Mr. Ramsey chose his words carefully, "A loose bolt caused the cable to give way."

Heather had caught him in a lie! *Maybe he has something to hide,* she considered. When the man left abruptly, Heather searched for contestants, hoping they would be more open. Just then she heard a commotion.

"Go ahead and quit!" someone shouted from the dressing room.

"Please be quiet!" came another voice.

"Maybe you want to keep your mouth shut, but I don't! Where's the press?" she asked loudly.

Several reporters rushed toward a glamorous young woman with thick, shiny brunette hair and almond-shaped green eyes.

"That's Ashley Pitman," one journalist said. "Now we might get some real news."

Although Heather joined them, she kept looking over her shoulder at the other model, a distraught-looking dark blonde clutching a bulging overnight bag.

She packed that in a hurry, Heather thought.

This contestant was also attracting attention. "Miss Neff," a reporter shouted. "Please, Miss Neff, I need to talk to you."

Kirsten Neff! Heather thought excitedly. *Just the person I want to see!*

A woman who looked like Kirsten's mother tried vainly to push the model through the throng.

"Just one question," a reporter pleaded.

Kirsten stopped in her tracks. "If I answer one, will you leave me alone?"

"Deal," he replied. "What happened to make you quit?"

Kirsten looked like a frightened deer. She pushed the man aside and ran out the lobby door.

Heather followed Kirsten, determined to know what was wrong. Just outside, Heather spotted a taxi driver and had a sudden inspiration. Jumping into the man's cab, she cried out, "Follow that car!"

3

A Foot in the Door

I charge extra for chases," the driver announced as Heather sat tensely on the back seat.

"Fine," she said, hoping she had enough money to pay him.

But there really was no chase. Kirsten's old station wagon plodded along, and the model had no idea she was being followed. Just past Norristown she turned off the road and into the parking lot of an aging motel.

"What now?" the man asked.

"Pull in the lot, but stay at a distance," Heather commanded. "Don't let them see you."

"Yes, Ma'am!" the cabby answered with a salute.

Heather watched Kirsten and the older woman go into their room. The taxi stopped a few doors away. The teenage reporter quickly paid the man and climbed out with her backpack. A few dilapidated houses stood near the motel.

This doesn't look like the place for a beauty queen, she thought, walking up to the door and knocking.

No one answered. Again she rapped on the door. "Miss Neff, I'm Heather Reed. I'd like to help you," she called out.

The door squeaked slightly open, and the older woman gave Heather a once-over. "Who did you say you were?" she asked in a heavy mid-western twang.

"I'm Heather Reed," she restated, "and I'd like to talk to Kirsten. I think I can help."

"Kirsten, do you know a Heather Reed?" she asked. The woman turned back to face Heather. "She says she doesn't know you."

The door started closing. The teenage reporter had to think fast. "That's such a shame," Heather blurted out. "Quitters have a hard time making it as models."

The woman hesitated, and Heather sensed that she was getting somewhere. "Kirsten will never get modeling assignments if she blows this."

"And what can you do about it?" asked Kirsten's guardian.

"I think I can convince her to stick with it."

That proved irresistible.

"Oh, come on in," the woman yielded. Heather entered quickly. "I'm Janet Mays, Kirsten's aunt."

"Nice to meet you," Heather said respectfully.

A bare overhead light shone harshly against cracked plaster walls and a road map of ceiling leaks. Faded quilts covered two twin beds. Makeup and perfume dominated a badly scratched chest of drawers. And in the midst of these shabby surroundings, Kirsten Neff sat on the edge of her bed like a deposed princess. Her eyes were swollen from crying.

"Hello, Miss Neff. I heard about your difficulties at the contest." Heather stood awkwardly, hoping one of them would invite her to sit down.

"Why should I trust you?" Kirsten asked suspiciously.

"Well, I'm covering the contest for *Star Struck* magazine, and I thought . . . "

Kirsten's brown eyes flashed. "You have a lot of nerve! Get out of here!" She stood up defiantly.

"Just give me one minute," Heather said calmly. "I may be a reporter, but I didn't come for an interview. If you tell me what's wrong, I can watch out for you."

Kirsten folded her arms and sat down. "Why would you do that? We don't even know each other."

Heather tried to explain without letting on that she was an amateur detective. "It would be a shame for you to drop out of the contest when your chances of winning are so good. But I especially don't want you to get hurt."

After a long moment Aunt Janet addressed her niece. "Maybe you ought to give her a chance. Remember your dad's condition," she whispered.

Kirsten closed her eyes, wrestling with her thoughts.

"Your dad?" Heather asked gently.

Janet nodded. "Kirsten entered the contest because she wants to be a big-time model and because the prize money would help pay some of the debts that have piled up since her daddy's accident. Times have been hard since my brother hurt his back."

Heather frowned. "I'm a little confused. Doesn't that mean you'd hate missing the contest?"

"Right, but I'm scared. It's a no-win situation," the young woman moaned.

"Please tell me why you're afraid," Heather coaxed. "I honestly want to help."

"Well, everything was wonderful when we got here three days ago," Kirsten began. "The contest officials treated me great. I got flowers and limousine rides and meetings with celebrities . . . "

"And fancy boxes of candy," Aunt Janet interrupted. "Now tell me, what model eats that stuff?"

For the first time since Heather arrived, the model smiled. Heather liked these two women.

"Anyway," Kirsten continued, "the judges and pageant officials paid special attention to me."

"They knew she was star material," Janet boasted.

"That must have been exciting," Heather said. "Have you modeled before?"

"Oh, just a little in Tulsa, Oklahoma. So you can imagine how big and important everything here seems."

Heather nodded. "So things went well at first."

Kirsten shivered. "Until yesterday. That's when I found a note backstage on my dressing table." She swallowed hard. "It said . . . " But she couldn't bring herself to say the words.

Aunt Janet had memorized it. "The note said, *'Go back to your farm home. Or you will never be a model again.'* It was written real funny-like."

"Was it signed?" Heather asked. Kirsten shook her head. "How did that part about the farm get in?"

"That's not hard," the model remarked. "Our biographies are fairly public."

"Who has access to them?" she inquired.

"The press, judges, other contestants," Kirsten said.

The teenager asked, "So you decided to quit?"

Kirsten inhaled deeply. "When we were on stage and that light fell, it nearly crushed Ashley Pitman," she explained. "I don't believe it was an accident."

"Why?" Heather asked. "Couldn't that light have fallen on anyone?"

"Ashley got a threatening note, too. And it just so happens we were all standing on assigned spots."

"Oh," Heather said. "Did you see Ashley's note?"

"No, but she told me about it. It said something about Humpty Dumpty falling down." Kirsten grimaced.

"Where's the one you got?" Heather asked.

"She tore it to pieces," Janet said.

"That's too bad," Heather responded. "But all isn't lost. Was it mailed or hand-delivered?"

Kirsten thought about it. "Hand-delivered, I think. Only my name was on the envelope."

"Was it written or typed?" Heather proceeded.

"Written, and the script was rather thick and bold," she recalled.

"Yeah," her aunt agreed. "It looked like a man's hand-writing."

"If you get another one, let me see it," Heather requested.

"There won't be another one," Kirsten's voice wavered. "I'm going home."

"I'm real worried, too," explained Janet, "but I think it would be a cryin' shame if you left now. Maybe this is all some prank."

"That's what I thought—until Ashley nearly got killed," Kirsten said emotionally.

"Someone may want to win so badly she's making empty threats to scare you away," Heather suggested.

"What about the stage light?" she pleaded. "That was no empty threat!"

"I'll check that out," Heather promised. "If someone is trying to hurt you and Ashley, that person must be stopped. Meanwhile, please don't go home yet."

"I don't know what you can do, but I won't go anywhere until I hear from you. Not even to tonight's rehearsal," Kirsten responded.

"Good. Just lay low tonight," Heather advised.

"Thank you," Janet said. "Sorry we were so hard on you at first."

"That's okay," Heather smiled. "I'll keep what you've told me private."

The teenager took another taxi back to the Music Fair at five-fifteen. The cabby had the radio on, and there was a report about the contest.

"Trouble is plaguing the American Model of the Year Contest," the announcer said. "In a photo session today at the Philadelphia Music Fair a light fell onto the stage, narrowly missing one of the competitors. In an earlier incident another competitor became ill and fainted. Contest coordinator Steven Ramsey says he's on the alert but expects things to quiet down."

At five-thirty Heather arrived at the Music Fair parking lot. She spotted the sporty, red sedan she and Brian shared. But instead of joining the gang, the amateur detective decided to look for Ashley Pitman first. Heather wanted to see Ashley's threatening note.

The teenager entered the lobby but stopped short when she heard two men arguing violently in the theater. The sound of what seemed to be a gunshot sent her diving behind a concession stand!

4

Another Accident?

When a Music Fair security guard rushed past Heather toward the theater, she quickly got up and followed. Inside, everything was chaos. Contestants screamed. TV reporters went live on early newscasts, and print journalists reached for their notebooks.

Heather spotted Chloé St. Johns and hurried to her side.

"Heather," she shouted. "I am so glad to see you!"

"Who got shot?" she asked.

"It was not a gun you heard," Chloé corrected. "A set fell off the stage and crashed into the orchestra pit. We are getting so jumpy around here!"

"But I heard some men yelling before the bang," Heather said.

The former model frowned. "The emcee, Nathan Drake, quarreled with Jean-Paul."

Heather noted the distasteful way she said the latter's name. "Why?"

"Mr. Drake wanted to do an interview about the

mishaps here, but Jean-Paul tried to talk him out of it," she explained.

"But it's public now," Heather commented. "Why would Jean-Paul mind if the emcee did an interview?"

"Because he does not want anyone else to receive publicity," Chloé said with contempt. "Jean-Paul also believes we should not over-publicize the problems." She paused. "I wish to tell you more about him, but now is not a good time. Can you meet me here tomorrow morning?"

"Yes."

"Very good! I would like to share with you some things I have learned about the mystery here," she said.

"I look forward to it," Heather responded eagerly. Then she asked, "Is Ashley Pitman around?"

"I saw her in the dressing room not long ago," Chloé remarked.

They said good-bye, and Heather went in search of Ashley. She found her sitting at her dressing table touching up her nail polish. When Heather introduced herself, the brunette looked her over to see if she was worthy of her time. Ashley had changed out of the party dress she been wearing earlier in the day at the photo session. But even in torn jeans, loafers, and a college sweatshirt, Ashley looked stunning. Her catlike, green eyes were spirited. Mrs. Pitman sat nearby looking equally glamorous in a smart-looking jumpsuit. Heather felt under-done.

"Mind if I ask a few questions?" the teenager said.

"Not at all," Ashley replied. She motioned Heather toward a chair like a queen granting a huge favor. "Of course, I am a bit distracted," she said, showing the girl her cherry-red nails. "I'm not used to doing this myself."

"Please tell me about the threatening note you received," Heather requested.

"What do you want to know?" she asked.

"When did you get it?"

"This morning," she said casually.

"What did it say?"

"Oh, something about Humpty Dumpty and knocking me off the wall," she said lightly.

"You're not concerned?" Heather raised her eyebrows.

"Why should I be?" The model sounded amused.

"Because the stage light almost knocked you out."

"Oh, that," she said, waving the nail polish brush.

"Do you think someone did it to scare you?" Heather suggested.

Mrs. Pitman spoke up. "Some people would do anything for $25,000."

"That much?" Heather asked.

"Plus a car and a modeling contract with America's top agency," Ashley replied.

"Which one is that?" the teenager inquired.

"The Castle Agency, of course," the model said.

Heather figured the obviously wealthy young woman was after the contract, not the money. "May I see the threatening message?" the girl asked.

"Mother will you check my garment bag? My nails are wet." Ashley blew on them for emphasis.

Mrs. Pitman went through the expensive bag and, after a few moments, found the note and showed it to

Heather. She examined the white vellum paper and matching envelope. The handwriting exactly resembled the thick style Kirsten and her aunt had described. On the envelope it simply said, "Ashley Pitman." Inside the message read, "Go back home, or like Humpty Dumpty you'll have a great fall."

The same unnatural language! Heather thought. *I wonder if it's Ashley's idea of a joke, or if there's some deeper meaning. Did she engineer this to make herself look innocent?*

"What do you think?" the model asked.

"Where did you find this?" Heather inquired.

"In my mail."

"And where do you pick that up?" she pursued.

"Mother, where do you get my mail?"

"In the green room," she explained, referring to where contestants waited before going on stage. "Each girl has a box."

Heather wondered whether a person from another country wrote the strange notes. But none of the contestants was foreign. Of course, two judges came from France, Chloé and Jean-Paul. *I can rule out Chloé,* she thought. Then the teenager remembered that Chloé had seemed upset with the French designer. Heather's thoughts raced as she tried to sort out the facts. *Both men and women are allowed in the green room, but Kirsten found her note on her dressing table. It seems more likely that a woman put it there.*

"Well?" Ashley demanded.

Heather came back to the present. "Are you thinking of pulling out?" she questioned.

"Goodness no!" she harrumphed. "I came to win, not get scared away by some silly note!" Then she checked her diamond-studded watch. "I have to meet another reporter now." Ashley got up and blew on her nails again. "Don't you want pictures before you go?"

"Uh, my photographer will arrive tomorrow," Heather stammered. "I'll get some then."

"Very well," Ashley said. "Come on, Mother."

Heather had been dismissed. She popped her notebook into her leather pack and headed for the Hot Spot. When she entered the popular restaurant, she strained on tiptoe to find Brian and her friends. Then her brother called out, "Heather!" from a nearby booth.

"What took you so long? We've been here an hour," Brian complained.

"She's sure not slow when it comes to food snatching," Joe commented dryly, as Heather helped herself to nachos from her brother's plate of appetizers.

A waitress came and took their orders, then Heather told Jenn and the guys everything that had happened.

"What a wild contest!" Joe exclaimed.

"Isn't it though?" Heather agreed. "Chloé wants me to meet her at the Music Fair early tomorrow morning. I think she has a suspect in mind. I can't wait to find out more!"

"Speaking of tomorrow," Jenn said. "I have to get to work by seven-thirty. Could you and Brian bring me?"

"Sounds good to me," Heather said.

"Joe and I don't need to be there until one o'clock," Brian stated. "I'm not getting there that early."

Heather thought for a moment. "Could you drive us to work, then keep the car?"

Brian grumbled. "I like sleeping in during spring break."

"Well, then, Dad can drop us off on his way to work," Heather decided.

"Much better," her brother replied.

After their meal all four teenagers ordered chocolate towers for dessert—vanilla ice cream and gooey hot fudge sauce topped with huge peaks of whipped cream. Then they waddled out to the parking lot.

"At times like these," Jenn remarked, "I'm glad not to be a model. Those women eat like mice." She sighed heavily. "But then they look so good."

"They sure do," Joe said, and Jenn punched him playfully on the arm.

As they made their way across the parking lot, Brian and Joe stopped to watch some teenagers rollerblading nearby. But Heather and Jenn continued on toward the car.

"Those guys are skating too close to people," Brian told his roommate.

"You're right," Joe agreed.

Suddenly one of the rollerbladers shot wildly out in front of the boys and seemed to deliberately head toward Heather and Jenn. Brian shouted and tried to warn them, but he was too late.

5

Strange Doings

The terrible collision sent Heather and Jenn to the ground. The impact also knocked the rollerblader off his feet, but only for a moment. In a flash he was back up and skating away. Brian and Joe ran angrily after him, but the skater quickly outdistanced them.

Joe continued after the rollerblader, while Brian rushed to Heather and Jenn.

"What happened?" Jenn asked, rubbing her right elbow. She sounded dazed.

"Some idiot on rollerblades ran you two over," he scowled. "Are you all right, Heather?"

His sister wiped gravel off her face. "I'm not sure everything is where it's supposed to be."

As Brian helped the two girls into the car, Joe returned looking unhappy.

"That jerk got away, and I didn't find any of his buddies, either," he moaned. "Are you girls okay?"

"I think we'll make it," Heather announced.

"Maybe so," Jenn replied, "but I'm one big ouch. Would I ever like to get my hands on that guy! What carelessness!"

"I doubt that was an accident," Heather remarked as Brian pulled out of the parking lot.

"You mean that creep ran into us on purpose?" Jenn asked in disbelief.

"Think about it for a minute. If it had been an accident, he would have stopped to see if we were hurt. Besides there are just too many strange things happening around here."

"But he was just a kid," Joe protested. "Anyway, why would anyone want to hurt you and Jenn?"

"I plan to find out," Heather vowed.

Fifteen minutes later they arrived home in the college town of Kirby, a Philadelphia suburb.

"I'll walk Jenn home," Brian said.

The McLaughlins lived across the street from the Reeds.

"Maybe Mom should look at her first," Heather suggested.

Mrs. Reed was a pediatrician and had an office in the basement of their home. Brian, Heather, and Jenn had gone to her with countless cuts and bruises.

"I'm okay, Heather," Jenn insisted. She started down the driveway, and Brian went with her.

"C'mon, Joe," Heather offered. "I'll go inside with you."

Joe's family had recently moved to Belgium when Mr. Rutli's company set up an operation in Brussels. But Joe stayed in the U.S. to go to college. Belgium was so far away, he could only see his family at Christmas and the summer break. Since he and Brian had become good friends, the Reeds told Joe to consider their home his. Sometimes Heather felt like she had two older brothers!

She and Joe walked through the enclosed side porch to the large kitchen.

"Mom, Dad, we're home!" she opened the door and called out.

"In the family room!" her mother responded from a distance.

Mr. and Mrs. Reed were curled up on the sofa reading and watching TV.

"I was just telling your mother all about your new adventure," her father said. But he stopped short upon seeing Heather's rumpled condition. "What in the world?" his voice trailed off.

Mrs. Reed immediately jumped up and inspected her daughter's facial cuts while Heather told the story.

"I wish I'd have caught that kid," Joe added as Brian came in.

"If y'all will excuse us, I'm going to get this young, uh, lady settled for the night," Mrs. Reed announced.

Upstairs Heather's mother treated the cuts. Then she helped her sixteen-year-old daughter into some comfortable pajamas.

"I feel so stiff," Heather complained.

"You probably will for a few days," Mrs. Reed replied. "Thank God this is all that happened."

Heather wasn't at all shaken. "It's so exciting, Mom! Tomorrow Chloé is going to tell me who she thinks is threatening the contestants."

"Why would someone do such a thing?" her mother frowned.

"One of them may be trying to knock others out the competition, or at least get them upset enough to do poorly," Heather offered. "Or someone else may have a stake in having a particular girl win." As the scratched and bruised teenager climbed into bed, she continued, "Mom, the winner will get $25,000, a new car, and a one-year contract with the Castle Modeling Agency."

"Those are incredible winnings!" Mrs. Reed exclaimed.

"I know. This case is going to be so exciting!"

Mrs. Reed sat on the side of Heather's bed and crossed her arms.

Uh oh, Heather thought. *I smell a lecture!*

"I wonder if your guardian angel ever gets tired," her mother laughed lightly. "I know it's difficult for you to stay out of mischief, darling, but do be careful. The last time you solved a mystery, you nearly got blown up. I worry about you, Heather."

"Mom, I'll be okay. And of course I'll be cautious," Heather promised. She looked down at the rabbit she kept in a cage in her room. "Has Murgatroid been fed?"

"She's your pet," Mrs. Reed reminded her.

The sixteen-year-old started to get out of bed, but her mother held her back.

"I'll do it this once. Just don't make it a habit."

After Mrs. Reed had fed the bunny and left the room, Heather called Kirsten Neff to see how she was doing. The model's aunt answered.

"Hello, this is Heather Reed. How are things going?" she asked.

"Good," Aunt Janet responded cheerfully.

"What's happened?" she asked eagerly.

"I'll let Kirsten tell you," she offered.

The model told Heather that Jean-Paul had called. "He said he felt badly about my dropping out and hoped I'd change my mind."

Heather thought it was unusual for the judge to take a personal interest in Kirsten. But she kept it to herself.

The next morning Mr. Reed called Heather from the doorway at five-thirty. She rolled over and stared at the clock in disbelief.

"What's going on?" she asked sleepily.

"If you and Jenn want a ride, you'll have to get up now," he said unsympathetically.

Heather sat up a little too quickly. "Ooh, I hurt all over," she whined.

But an hour later she was outside greeting Jenn. Her friend looked stylish in black jeans, a red and black plaid shirt, and her black leather jacket.

"A comfortable, fashionable look for a model's assistant," Heather approved.

Her own clothes were slightly more dressed-up. She wore pink stirrup pants, a fuzzy pink sweater, and a bright orange blazer. Heather's long, honey-brown hair was held back with a multi-colored bow.

Mr. Reed dropped the teens off at a family restaurant within walking distance of the Music Fair. They hadn't eaten yet and didn't need to report to work for another forty-five minutes.

Later, on the way to their new jobs, Jenn said she felt nervous. "What if I spill something on them or act stupid?" she worried.

"You won't," Heather reassured her friend.

Jenn hugged her gratefully, and they both moaned with pain. Then they laughed, but that hurt too! Their eyes scanned the parking lot for the rollerbladers. To their relief, there were no skaters anywhere.

When Jenn reported to her bosses, Heather looked for Chloé St. Johns in the theater area. Instead she bumped into Kirsten Neff.

"It's so nice to see you!" the teenage reporter exclaimed.

"It's good to be back," the model smiled graciously.

Just then Steven Ramsey announced over the loudspeaker, "Ladies, please report to the dressing room immediately."

"See you later," she said and hurried off.

Heather spotted Chloé standing near the sound booth.

She was talking to a handsome man in his early twenties.

"Heather, good morning! I'm glad you're here so early," she said. "I'd like you to meet Eric Kressler from *Star Struck*. Eric, this is Heather Reed."

The young man's blue eyes were clear and sharply accented by curly black hair. At six feet, he towered over the petite teenager.

This guy is gorgeous! Heather thought, absently shaking hands with him.

"I'm looking forward to working with you," Eric said, flashing a dazzling smile. "I hear this contest is pretty exciting."

"It sure is!" Heather agreed.

Just then Jenn ran into the theater and yelled breathlessly, "Who owns a white BMW?"

Chloé called out, "I do."

"You'd better come right away," Jenn said urgently.

6

Slashed Tires

Chloé rushed to the parking lot with the young people on her heels. When they got to her BMW, the former model gasped. The white sedan was sadly resting on its rims. Someone had slashed all four tires! Eric began snapping pictures.

"When did you notice this?" Chloé asked Jenn.

"A few minutes ago," she said, winded. "When I went to the mobile diner to get pastries for Marci and Luke, I saw someone run away from the car."

Chloé inspected the damage as Eric continued taking photos. She looked at him with annoyance, but he didn't notice. He was clearly in his element. The sound of the commuter train running behind the Music Fair filled the air.

"What did the slasher look like?" Heather asked her friend, straining to be heard over the noise.

"I didn't get a good look," she commented. "But he seemed about our age, and thin."

"Hair color?" the teenage sleuth continued.

"Um, dark. I didn't get a good look at his face."

"I'm going to call the police," Chloé announced, picking up her car phone. Then she phoned her garage for a tow truck.

While they waited for the police, Heather wondered what connection this incident might have to the mystery. *Now I'm really anxious to know what Chloé wanted to tell me this morning. Someone must either be trying to distract her or to scare her off their trail.*

When two police officers arrived, Chloé and Jenn answered their questions.

"This is some contest!" the policewoman remarked. "If I were you, I'd be extra careful around here."

Then the tow truck pulled up. Before she left with it, Chloé told Heather privately, "We still need to talk."

"Later today?" the teenager asked hopefully.

"It depends on how long it takes to get the tires replaced. Then I must finish an assignment for the newspaper." She lowered her voice. "Keep your eyes wide open, Heather."

"What do you mean?" she asked, tilting her head.

But the tow truck's driver waved Chloé inside, and she left.

"I got some great shots!" Eric boasted.

Heather frowned disapprovingly. "I think you could've been more sensitive."

"My job is to take pictures," he shrugged.

"I'd better go back," Jenn said. "Marci and Luke are probably wondering what's taking me so long."

"I'm sure they'll understand," Heather soothed.

"I'm not," her friend called over her shoulder as she hurried away.

Eric turned his winning blue eyes on Heather. "What's next, pretty one?"

She dismissed his effort to appease her. "I'd like to coordinate our activities," she said.

They went to the press room and discussed what their editor, Rhonda Cowley, wanted their coverage to include.

"The first thing she wants you to do is interview the finalists," Eric stated.

"All of them?" Heather gulped.

"How many are there?" he questioned.

"There will be ten. Right now, twenty-five girls are competing."

"How about talking to the top five contenders?" he suggested. "You can tell who they are by listening to conversations while you work. When will the finalists be chosen?"

"I'm not sure," Heather said.

"Well, just talk to the five. I'll photograph them, then we'll fax the interviews to Rhonda," he said. "Let's get to work!"

They went to the theater and chose seats next to Steven Ramsey and Joan Winchell. A band played in the orchestra pit, and the models practiced walking the aisles surrounding the circular platform.

"How long will this take?" Heather asked Mr. Ramsey.

"Another fifteen minutes," he said.

"Then will they be free?" she asked.

"They'll get a thirty-minute break before the next activity." He gave Heather an irritated look. "Didn't you get today's schedule from the press room?"

"I'm afraid not," she admitted. "Did you, Eric?"

He shook his head.

"Here," Joan Winchell handed her a copy. "You can pick a new one up every morning in the press room."

"Thank you. Chloé St. Johns was going to show me around this morning, but she had to get her car fixed."

"I heard about that," Steven remarked. "That's a shame."

You don't sound very sympathetic, Heather thought. She wondered what motive he might have to threaten the contestants, and decided to keep an eye on him. Then she examined the press release. The modeling hopefuls would have a thirty-minute press conference after their break. Then they would go to the Main Line Mall to model summer fashions for Tenley's Department Store. In addition Heather learned the finalists would be chosen the following night.

Since everyone expected Kirsten and Ashley to make the top ten, Heather decided to interview them. When the practice session ended, the young women streamed toward the dressing area. Heather caught Kirsten's eye and motioned for her to wait.

"Hi, Kirsten! You look great out there!"

"Thank you." The model's warm brown eyes seemed to smile. "You've been so nice." She pointed to Eric. "I see you have a helper today."

"Kirsten Neff, meet Eric Kressler from *Star Struck*," she said. They shook hands, then Heather asked if she could interview the model.

"Sure," she said. Then she lowered her voice. "But not about the stuff we discussed yesterday."

"It's a deal," Heather agreed. "Let's go outside. Eric says the light's good for taking pictures."

"Hey! What about me?" a voice called from behind them.

They turned to see Ashley Pitman. The tall brunette tossed her dark, wavy hair. "I hope *Star Struck* has the good sense to interview me." She winked boldly at Eric.

"Of course," Heather said with forced politeness. "Come with us." *Maybe I can pick up some clues,* the teenage detective thought.

As they walked outside, Ashley asked coyly, "And who is this handsome hunk?"

The photographer laughed. "A woman who speaks her mind!" he remarked.

"Ashley, this is Eric Kressler. Eric, meet Ashley Pitman."

"I'm going to win this contest," she announced.

"Is that right?" he asked with a chuckle.

"Where's your aunt?" Heather asked Kirsten. She wanted to change the subject before getting totally nauseated.

"She went shopping at the mall," Kirsten explained.

"That's where my mother went," Ashley commented. "She needs a new dress for the big night."

"Maybe my aunt will run into her," her opponent said kindly.

"I doubt it," Ashley responded. "My mother is looking for something expensive." Kirsten's shoulders slumped.

Ashley, Heather thought, *you seem to have everything but manners! Is this cruelty of yours intended to wear Kirsten down?*

"What made you change your mind about leaving?" the stuck-up model asked her rival.

"There was no need to leave," the pretty blonde answered simply.

"That's the spirit!" Ashley exclaimed. "Now I have some real competition."

Kirsten scrunched her thick eyebrows. "What do you mean by that?"

"The other contestants are nothing. You're the only one with enough flair to challenge me. I do want some suspense," she explained.

Eric laughed, and Heather elbowed him in the ribs. "It's not funny," she scolded.

They set to work taking pictures and asking questions. At one point Jenn came outside looking frazzled. She quietly sat at a distance while her friend worked.

Heather learned that besides some modeling, Kirsten also worked as a manicurist. The vibrant Ashley, on the other hand, came from a wealthy California family. Her mother had been an actress in her youth, and according to Ashley, Mr. Pitman ran a major import business.

When the interviews ended, Eric and Heather arranged to meet later. Heather went over to where Jenn was sitting. "You seem bushed," she observed.

"I am!" she groaned. "And I don't like Marci and Luke after all. They're running me ragged. 'Get this!' 'Get that!' They act like I'm their slave or something." She sighed. "And these bruises from yesterday are too much."

"So much for Luke Granger," Heather remarked.

"You bet!" Jenn exclaimed. "Now about that Eric Kressler . . . " Her voice trailed off.

"I thought you'd like him," Heather teased.

"Don't you?"

"He is gorgeous," Heather agreed. "But he's also a little too impressed with himself."

The two friends were starting to climb the steps to the Music Fair when they heard someone yell, "Wait up!" It was Brian and Joe.

For several minutes Heather and Jenn told them about their experiences so far that day.

"Such excitement!" Brian commented. Then, checking his watch, he said, "We'd better get to work."

"And I'd better get to the press conference!" Heather said. She arrived in the theater just as it started. Joan Winchell handed her a packet of biographies on each contestant and pointed out a seat for Heather to take.

This is great! Heather thought. *These biographies will make my work easier and leave me more time to solve the mystery.*

The half-hour event went smoothly. Since most of the contestants' answers sounded alike, Heather let her mind wander. She still believed Ashley could have made the threats to upset the other contestants and give her an advantage. But it didn't seem likely that the model would have set up the rollerblading accident or the tire slashing. And it didn't make sense for a contender to want to alienate a judge. *She also doesn't seem to know I'm only a substitute reporter,* Heather considered.

Steven Ramsey's voice interrupted Heather's thoughts. "Thank you for your time," he began. "I think . . . " He stopped abruptly. A good-looking man in his late twenties had strutted onto the stage and rudely snatched the microphone from the contest coordinator's hands.

"Hello, ladies and gentlemen," the intruder said, flashing a brilliant smile.

"Who's that?" Heather asked Alan Pima, a TV reporter sitting next to her.

"That's Nathan Drake," he said soberly. "There's going to be trouble now."

7

Jealous Competitors

I've never heard of him," Heather said.

Alan regarded her in disbelief. "You've never heard of . . . Oh, forget it," he shrugged. "You're too young to remember 'Scobey.'"

"'Scobey,'" the teenager repeated. "Wasn't that the show about a boy and his pet bear?"

"That's the one."

"I've seen it on reruns," Heather told him. "You mean Nathan Drake starred as the little boy?"

"Uh huh."

"What's he doing here?" she asked.

"He's the emcee. Nathan does beauty contests now . . . and game shows," the TV reporter added. "He's on 'Shop or Drop.' Pretty grim if you ask me. His whole career since 'Scobey' has been bleak."

"What do you mean?" asked Heather.

"He made some rotten pictures a few years ago." Alan laughed cynically. "One involved rabid ducks."

Heather watched the well-dressed, well-built man prance about the stage. "He does have a strong presence," she commented.

She could tell Steven Ramsey was angry as he muttered something to Drake and stomped off the stage.

"It wasn't very nice of Nathan Drake to upstage Mr. Ramsey like that," Heather concluded. "Why don't they like each other?"

"Ramsey thinks the coordinator should handle the press. But Nathan wants to be the center of attention."

Then Alan Pima got up to leave, but Heather stopped him. "Just one more thing," she said. "Does Pep Shampoo employ both of them?"

"Technically," he said. "But Drake's only on the payroll for this contest."

"What about Marci Bentley and Luke Granger?"

"They're like Drake—'faces.'"

"Excuse me?" She didn't understand.

"They're here promotionally. On the night of the contest, they'll do live commercials." Then Alan added, "I don't blame Ramsey. I overheard the Music Fair manager say Pep Shampoo gave him a raw deal."

Heather frowned. "A raw deal?"

"Yeah. Ramsey does the grunt work, and Drake gets the glory." Alan motioned toward his cameraman and said, "I have to run. See you again soon."

"Bye!" The teenager sank into her seat to think over the situation. *So, Steven Ramsey has a motive after all.*

Maybe he wants to undermine the contest to punish Pep Shampoo, she pondered.

"Heather!" Jenn broke into her thoughts.

"Hi, Jenn! What's going on?"

"This job is no fun," she sighed.

"All work and no play?" Heather guessed.

"You bet! Marci and Luke constantly drink mineral water and read about themselves in magazines. Guess who goes after the mineral water and magazines?"

"You," Heather smiled.

"And clean up after them?" Jenn continued.

"You again." Heather patted the seat next to her. "Come and sit for a few minutes."

"Chair? What's a chair? Sit? No such thing," the red-head stated. "I just came by to tell you I can't ride to the mall with you and the guys. Luke and Marci want me nearby. I'm like a genie; you know, their wish is my command, and all that stuff."

"I hope it gets better," Heather said.

"Me too." Then Jenn asked, "So, who's the chief suspect?"

Heather put a finger to her lips. "I don't want anybody to know."

"Sorry," Jenn clapped a hand over her mouth.

"Actually I'm still in the early stages." She didn't want to discuss the case in public.

"I'll wait until we're alone," Jenn said, lowering her voice. "But if you want my opinion, I think that jerk Ashley Pitman is up to no good."

Suddenly Marci Bentley's voice rang out, "Jenn! Jenn!"

"See what I mean?" she asked. "I'm coming!" Jenn yelled.

Heather laughed. "Poor girl! Oh, well. I'd better find the guys."

She spotted Brian and Joe in the lobby. They were carrying their clothes for the fashion show and did not look happy.

"Man, these are the stupidest get-ups I've ever seen!" Joe complained.

"I hope no one recognizes me," Brian commented.

"What's the problem?" Heather unzipped the garment bag. In it were a gaudy cowboy costume and an Elvis-type jumpsuit. "Oh," she said.

"We could refuse," Joe stated.

"And lose our jobs," Brian added sensibly.

"Is it worth your self-respect?" his roommate challenged.

Brian grinned. "No, but it is worth that new tent I've been wanting."

Joe bit his lower lip. "And it may be worth ski boots." He thought for a moment. "I'll do it, but can't we wear fake noses and mustaches?"

"At least your classmates are out of town for spring break," Heather comforted.

When they emerged from the dimly lit theater, Heather reveled in the brilliant blue sky and the sound of robins singing happily. But another noise—that of rollerbladers—captured her attention. "Where's that coming from?" she asked.

"Over by the restaurant," Brian remarked. "Let's find out who they are."

Heather made out the figures of three males. But she had trouble learning more because they moved quickly and wore helmets. When they spotted Heather and her companions, they hurried behind the Hot Spot and disappeared.

"Rats!" Heather exclaimed.

"Maybe we'll get another chance to find out who they are," Joe said.

"If someone with the contest is paying them, they'll keep hanging around," he predicted.

When Heather and the boys reached Tenley's Department Store, Brian and Joe reported to dressing rooms in the men's department. Heather soon found Eric Kressler near the runway. He was taking pictures of the contestants as they checked out the stage. Then Joan Winchell herded all the models backstage. Kirsten Neff saw Heather and smiled weakly. Heather thought the model looked extremely pale.

"Let's follow them," Eric said. "I want to get backstage pictures, too."

As the photographer and teenage reporter walked backstage with the models, Heather couldn't help feeling anxious for Kirsten. Eric chattered continually about the great pictures he was taking. Then Heather picked up the sound of Steven Ramsey's angry voice.

"Shh!" Heather nudged Eric.

"I don't see why he keeps upstaging me," the coordinator growled. "He's doing it on purpose."

"He's an idiot!" Joan Winchell hissed.

"He'll pay for it," Steven vowed sullenly.

Heather and Eric stared at each other. "It doesn't get more obvious than that," the young man said. "This contest is so tense!"

"There's a great deal to be won or lost here," Heather replied vaguely.

Just then an older woman approached them. "Hello, Eric. I believe you've met my daughter, Courtney Lewis." She took the blonde, green-eyed beauty by the shoulders and propelled her toward them. "These lovely folks are with *Star Struck* magazine," she gushed.

Heather said hello. Although she had seen the Lewises around, she hadn't spoken with them. Courtney was about nineteen or twenty and naturally pretty.

Her mother was just the opposite. Of average height, Mrs. Lewis's white-blonde hair was styled in a sophisticated pageboy. Her clothes were immaculately tailored, and she wore so much silver jewelry it gave her a shimmery appearance. Her perfume made Heather's eyes water.

"You look nice enough to enter the contest yourself," Eric said brightly.

A strange look crossed the woman's face. "That's very kind of you," she answered. "You'll find my Courtney the best-dressed of the competitors."

Just then a dark-haired contestant bumped absently into Courtney. "Oh, excuse me!" she apologized.

"Only graceful young ladies should be allowed to compete," Mrs. Lewis said harshly.

Her daughter looked down, embarrassed by her mother's outburst.

"Who was that?" Eric asked.

Courtney wanted to erase the impression her mother's unkind words had made. "That's Laura LaMonica," she said. "I'm sure she'll be a finalist."

"I doubt that!" Mrs. Lewis huffed. "It's amazing what rabble Pep Shampoo brought into this contest." She smiled broadly at Eric and Heather, "Be sure to take lots of good pictures of Courtney!" Then she whisked the young woman away.

"I'll be glad when this is over!" Eric stated.

Heather consulted her watch. "We'd better find our places. The show starts in five minutes."

As if to underscore her words, Steven Ramsey announced, "Okay, ladies! Let's go!"

Joan Winchell lined up the models and escorts in their proper order. Heather saw Brian and waved. He looked obviously pleased to be on Kirsten Neff's arm in spite of his Elvis outfit. Joe stood further back with a petite blonde whose curly hair seemed almost as long as she was tall.

Heather and Eric walked briskly through the store's lower level, now off-limits to customers. Although the area was mobbed, they found seats in a row marked "Press Only."

Nathan Drake hopped onto the stage wearing an Italian designer suit. His toothy smile immediately won the audience. They applauded, and he basked in the attention.

"Thank you, thank you," he said, trying to calm them down, though not too hard. "Welcome to The Summer Fashion Extravaganza presented by Tenley's Department Store and Pep Shampoo. The women you'll see are participants in the American Model of the Year Contest sponsored by Pep Shampoo. Tomorrow ten finalists will be announced, and the following evening the winner will be chosen in a concluding ceremony at the Philadelphia Music Fair. We invite you to attend this thrilling event. And now here are America's hottest models, Marci Bentley and Luke Granger!"

The popular duo looked sensational as they stepped onto the stage amid thunderous applause.

"I'll bet Jenn's glad to be rid of them for a few minutes," Heather whispered to Eric. He laughed and nodded vigorously.

Laura LaMonica and her escort started the show. Laura was wearing a stunning short dinner dress of blue sequins. It looked fantastic against her dark hair.

Then Kirsten came out with Brian. She sported a smart denim outfit. But the young woman had a funny look on her face, and her walk was unsteady. Kirsten forced a smile as she moved down the runway. Heather thought her new friend was getting too close to the edge of the stage. Suddenly the blonde model's heel got caught in a crack, and she stumbled. Kirsten was going to fall!

8

Mysterious Illness

The audience gasped, and Brian lunged forward, grabbing Kirsten's arm. His quick action kept her from falling. But then the poor girl went limp, so he carried her back to the dressing area.

"I'll be back," Heather told Eric, jumping up from her seat. Two female reporters joined her. A security officer detained them, even after they flashed their press badges. Once he finally let them inside the store, Heather spotted Brian. He had just left Kirsten with her Aunt Janet and some paramedics.

"What happened?" Heather asked breathlessly. The other newswomen also prodded him for information.

"I'm not sure," he responded. "Kirsten said she had a stomachache."

Steven Ramsey walked over to them with a clipboard. "Brian, please get ready to go back out."

"But, what about Kirsten?" he protested.

"You've done all you can. Find your next model," the contest coordinator said.

"I'll stay here," Heather assured him.

Her brother nodded and reluctantly returned to his work in the fashion show. Moments later ambulance attendants took a very sick Kirsten away.

Heather spotted Kirsten's aunt and ran to her. "Excuse me, Janet. Do they know what's wrong?"

"No, but Kirsten has to go to the hospital. She's awful sick, Heather." The woman cried softly.

The teenager quickly wrote down her phone number. "Please call me at home tonight," she requested. "I want to know how Kirsten gets along."

"I will," Janet promised as she hurried away. Just then Jenn joined Heather.

"Got any clues to what's going on?" the red-head asked.

"I'm not sure," Heather replied.

"Do you think someone made Kirsten sick?" her friend asked, wide-eyed.

"It sure seems that way," Heather said grimly.

Both girls watched the rest of the fashion show on the backstage monitor, but it was difficult to concentrate.

When the show finally ended, Brian and Joe quickly changed into street clothes. Heather met briefly with Eric, and Jenn did some last-minute running around for Marci Bentley. Then the foursome caught up with each other just outside Tenley's main entrance.

"I never saw anyone use so much hair spray!" Jenn complained. "No wonder Marci never has a hair out of place!" Then she added, "I'm starved! Is anybody else hungry?"

Suddenly Heather snapped her fingers.

"What is it?" her brother asked in annoyance. "I hate it when you do that."

"I left my backpack in the dressing area, and my wallet's in it. Wait here."

The teenager hurried back to Tenley's and found her pack near a water fountain. She slung it over her shoulder and started walking away when the sound of a man and woman talking secretively nearby caught her attention.

"Things will be a lot simpler now," the woman said quietly. "Now we only have one to worry about."

Though the woman's voice sounded familiar, Heather couldn't place it. Nor could she hear the man's response. When she gathered enough courage to go around the wall that separated her from them, Heather sighed. They were gone!

Too bad! she thought. Then Heather realized, *This part of the store isn't open to shoppers yet, so those people had to be associated with the contest.*

She looked around for any clues that might give her a lead on the identity of the couple. The lingering scent of Chantal perfume hung in the air where the couple had talked. Chantal was a popular frangrance. It wasn't much of a clue, but it was better than nothing.

Heather determined to find out which women associated with the contest also wore Chantal. Then she rejoined her brother and friends and told them what had happened.

"Now I *know* someone made Kirsten sick!" Brian slapped a fist into the palm of his other hand.

They discussed the mystery on their way to the food court, agreeing foul play was surely involved in Kirsten's sudden ailment. But who was responsible? All of them suspected Ashley. Privately Heather wasn't so sure. It seemed too easy.

That night the phone rang while she was sitting on her bedroom floor, playing with Murgatroid, her pet rabbit.

"Oh, thank you for calling!" the teenager said when she heard Janet Mays' voice. Janet was calling from Suburban Hospital. "How is Kirsten?"

"She's real sick," came the response.

"What is it?" Heather held her breath.

"The doctor said she has food poisoning. He's afraid of letting her go back to the motel tonight, so we'll stay here."

"Have you been eating at the same places as Kirsten?" the teenager asked.

Janet seemed puzzled by the question. "Uh, yes, I think so. Why?"

Heather knew that when one person became ill from food, usually others did as well. She suspected Kirsten's illness had been deliberately caused, but she didn't want to alarm the woman. "I'm just curious," Heather explained.

Then Janet cried out, "We should have left town yesterday. As soon as she can go, we're leaving!"

Although Heather couldn't blame her, she hoped Janet wouldn't take Kirsten home yet.

"Please don't blame yourself," she soothed. Then she added, "I'm praying for Kirsten."

"Thank you," the woman replied. "You've been so kind. We appreciate all you're trying to do."

When Heather hung up, she quickly located the names of several area hospitals in the phone book. Then she called each of their emergency rooms and asked whether they had treated food poisoning victims that day. None of them had. Because of that and the hushed conversation she'd overheard after the fashion show, Heather became convinced foul play was involved.

"What's your theory, Murgatroid?" she asked her pet.

The phone interrupted her reflections. It was Jenn. When she learned about Kirsten's food poisoning, she agreed it sounded strange. "I hope you solve this mystery fast!" she exclaimed. "I'm getting the creeps!"

Heather went to the family room where everyone was watching the news. During a commercial she told them about Kirsten's condition.

"I'll bet it was intentional," Brian said grimly. "Normally I wouldn't say that, but too much has happened."

"Same here," Joe chimed in.

"That contest is getting out-of-hand!" Mrs. Reed concluded with a shudder.

The phone rang again, and Heather answered it. "Hello? Oh, hello, Chloé! I'm really glad you called. Did you hear about Kirsten? On the radio? Her aunt just told me it was food poisoning. You would? Terrific!" A moment later she hung up and announced, "Chloé's coming right over. She has something big to tell me."

"I wish you would've asked, Heather," her mother sighed. "Just look at this mess! Newspapers and magazines everywhere!" She immediately began straightening up while everyone else just sat there. "Come on people!" she ordered impatiently.

Fifteen minutes later the front doorbell rang. Heather quickly stuffed an empty soft drink can under the couch, then ran to answer the door.

"I hope you do not mind my coming on such short notice," Chloé told the Reeds as they came into the living room to greet her.

"Not at all," Mr. Reed said quickly, taking Chloé's long leather coat.

"And please do not be further offended by my need to speak with Heather alone," the former model said.

"That's quite all right," Patrick Reed said. With that, he and his wife returned to the family room.

Heather took Chloé to the den. "So, what's up?"

The woman's amber eyes looked troubled as she nervously fingered the strap of her expensive purse. "I know who is threatening the contestants!" she exclaimed.

9

Star Reporter

Tell me everything!" Heather begged.

"Jean-Paul is doing these terrible things!" Chloé explained.

"Why do you think so?" the teenager inquired.

"I have known him a long time," she began. "And he has always been shifty. So when things began to go wrong with the contest, I immediately suspected him. But I had nothing concrete to go by until my tires were slashed," she said certainly.

"You're saying he's dishonest?" Heather asked.

"Oh, yes!" she exclaimed. "Jean-Paul's designs were what you call 'the rage' in Paris when I was modeling. I was excited when he asked me to represent his creations at a major exposition. But the arrangement went sour."

"What happened?" asked Heather.

Chloé grimaced. "One day quite by mistake I discovered he was passing off a young Italian girl's outfits as his. He was a fake!"

"Wow! What did you do?"

"I refused to model his clothes," Chloé remarked. "He said I would never work again."

"How awful!" the teenager sympathized. "But you did work. And he's famous. How did that come about?"

"Because we knew his secret, my agent said we would ruin his reputation if he put me out of work." The beautiful woman paused. "There has been an uneasy truce between us since then."

"So, you think Jean-Paul wrecked your car and threatened the models," Heather summarized.

"And had you knocked down by that rollerblader," Chloé interrupted.

Heather regarded her with wide eyes. "Do you have any evidence?"

"Not directly," she admitted. "But think about it. Jean-Paul pays people to do his dirty work. And he's always been on guard with me, waiting for me to go public with my knowledge of him."

"So he would want to get you out of the way," the girl said. "And he might know about our friendship. But isn't paying those boys to hurt me and Jenn too obvious?" The teenager twisted some hair around her index finger.

Chloé shook her head. "He's not very smart."

"Okay. What made you hurry over here tonight?"

"When I learned Kirsten Neff had food poisoning, I became frantic," the ex-model replied. I had to tell you about Jean-Paul before he tries something even worse!"

"You know what's really weird?" Heather asked. "He called Kirsten the other night to convince her not to drop out of the competition."

Chloé was amazed. "He phoned her?"

"Uh huh," the teenager affirmed.

"Then he did so for a dark reason," she murmured.

"What do you think it is?" Heather asked.

"I believe he wants to snatch up the winner and get her to model his designs," Chloé stated. "This is a very important contest in the fashion industry. Jean-Paul's popularity has lagged in recent years. This may be the boost he needs to get back on top."

"Does that mean he would try to advance his favorite in the competition?" the girl inquired.

"I think so," she nodded.

Heather took a deep breath. "At first I thought he was partial to Kirsten because of that phone call. But now that she's mysteriously sick, the call may have been a cover-up," she sighed. "But maybe there's more than one mystery here."

Then Heather told Chloé about the conversation she'd overheard at Tenley's after the fashion show. The woman was furious.

"So if it were Jean-Paul you heard, he is working with a woman. But whom?"

"And why?" Heather added. "Chloé, there are still others who could be acting dishonestly. For instance, Steven Ramsey is very upset about Pep Shampoo's treatment of him. And Nathan Drake craves the publicity he had when he was younger. Then there's Ashley Pitman, who insists she's going to win."

"This is not going to be easy," Chloé said. "But your assignment with *Star Struck* will help. You'll have access to everyone involved with the contest. Please let me know if I can be of more help."

"Thank you," the teenager said.

The tall woman picked up her purse and rose to leave.

"Would you like to visit with my family awhile before you go?" She added impishly, "My mom will think straightening up was worth the effort."

"Of course," she laughed. "Perhaps I could have a cup of tea."

"I'll bet Mom's already made it," Heather stated. "She gets all worked up over company."

The Reeds, Joe, and Chloé chatted over refreshments for an hour. The fashion editor filled them in on some thoughts she had shared with Heather.

The following day the teenager got up early and drove to the Music Fair with Brian and her friends.

"This is going to be a really busy day," Joe announced, yawning.

"You seem tired already," Jenn teased.

"This modeling stuff isn't as easy as it looks," he complained. "It's so tedious."

"Don't I know it!" Jenn lamented.

Heather giggled in spite of herself. "Not too pleased with Marci and Luke, are we?" she asked.

"No, we are not. I will never idolize a celebrity again. They're just like everyone else—only worse," she exclaimed. The others laughed.

Fifteen minutes later Brian pulled the red sedan he shared with his sister into the Music Fair parking lot.

"Look at all the cars!" Brian observed.

"I'll bet those vans are for transporting the contestants to center city," Jenn mentioned. She pointed to a fleet of brightly-colored vehicles.

A photo opportunity for the contestants was scheduled at Philadelphia's historic area for late morning. Rhonda Cowley had told Heather there was no need to write a story about it. She only wanted pictures.

Heather got out of the car and looked around for the rollerbladers. None were around.

Inside the Music Fair Jenn searched for Marci and Luke, and the guys looked up Steven Ramsey to get their instructions. Heather went to the press room and read the daily news release.

"What a busy day!" Alan Pima exclaimed.

"It sure will be," the teenager agreed.

"I'm up to it!" Eric Kressler approached them cheerfully. He looked very pleased about something.

"Good morning," Heather said. "You seem happy!"

"I am," he replied, pouring himself a cup of coffee. "It's going to be a fun day."

They reviewed their agenda, then Heather excused herself to check on Kirsten's condition. "I'm going out to make a private phone call," she said, avoiding the public ones in their newsroom.

"The press meets the judges in five minutes," Eric pointed to the wall clock.

"I'll make it short," Heather promised.

She went to the lobby and called Suburban Hospital.

"I'm glad to hear from you," the contestant's aunt told Heather. "Kirsten's much better this morning."

"I'm relieved to hear that," the teenage reporter said sincerely. "Will she make the finals tonight?"

"She'll be ready by then. You may not believe this," Janet said, "but Kirsten's more determined than ever to be there. She's not going to let anything stop her now." She sounded pleased with her niece's attitude.

"That's fantastic!" Heather couldn't contain her relief.

"And I'm not going to let anyone hurt her again," Janet vowed. "They'll have to get me first." Then she became sober. "You know, Kirsten insists she ate the same thing everbody else did yesterday."

Now Heather was certain it had been deliberate. She thanked Janet for the information and hurried back to the press conference. Eric motioned from his second-row seat for her to join him. Then Steven Ramsey took the stage.

"These are the ladies and gentlemen who will choose ten finalists this evening for the American Model of the

Year Contest. Tomorrow night they will select one winner from that group. Feel free to ask any questions you
might have."

Chloé St. Johns, looking radiant in a gold-colored suede
suit, smiled in Heather's direction. The teenager nodded
at her as the coordinator introduced the judges. Five of
them, including Chloé, worked in the media. Heather was
surprised to see her favorite national anchorwoman,
Frances Sansom, among them. One judge hosted a popular afternoon dance show on cable. Then there was the
owner of a fashionable clothing store chain, a museum
curator, a U.S. senator, a football player, and Jean-Paul.
Steven Ramsey gave him a big build-up.

"Finally, we have with us the world's most popular
designer, Jean-Paul."

The sophisticated Frenchman basked in the acclaim.
"I am thrilled to be part of this competition," he smiled
broadly. The middle-aged man looked every bit the fashion designer in a beautifully-tailored suit and hand-sewn
shoes. His mustache was neatly trimmed and his hair, cut
with precision. "In Paris we have high hopes for the
winner. It will be an honor to help choose her."

"What kind of hopes?" one reporter shouted.

"She will be an international trend-setter in the fashion industry," he beamed with excitement.

Heather exchanged a surprised glance with Chloé as
the reporter persisted. "Is that because the fashion business has been so unpopular lately?"

A ripple of laughter spread across the room. At first Jean-Paul sneered, but he quickly put his winning smile back in place.

"In a way, yes," he replied. "Most designers have produced absurd clothes that even models cannot make attractive. But the American Model of the Year will be fresh and appealing. She will create a new era in the fashion industry."

Heather's mouth dropped open. It seemed Chloé St. Johns was dead right about him!

10

Heather's Hunch

At the reception afterward, Chloé discreetly whispered to Heather, "Now I am sure."

The girl nodded, then mixed casually with the other judges, including Jean-Paul. She wanted the opportunity to speak with him directly.

"I have heard of your magazine," he told her. "You must be quite good to work at so young an age." His voice held a note of sarcasm.

"Thank you," Heather said stiffly. "There are so many wonderful contestants. I don't know how you will possibly make such a difficult choice."

"There are ways, *ma cherie*," he smiled thinly. Then he bowed and excused himself.

What ways? Heather wondered darkly.

The judges began leaving. Heather still had a little time to investigate Kirsten's food poisoning before the vans left for center city.

Heather's first stop was the dressing area where

models agonized over their appearances. *I wonder how they pay for all their outfits?* she wondered.

Modeling hopeful Laura LaMonica interrupted Heather's thoughts. "Do you know if Kirsten Neff will make the finals?" she asked in genuine concern.

"Yes," she smiled. "Her aunt says she'll be there tonight."

Ashley Pitman sniffed. "It's a wonder. She's such a baby."

Then Heather realized something: *Ashley's almost too obvious to be a real suspect.*

She paused near the model's dressing table. Although she was a snob, Ashley liked to talk, and Heather had an important question on her mind.

"How do contestants afford all these clothes?" she inquired. "That's quite an expense!"

The model applied another coat of mascara to her already-dazzling eyelashes. "Most of them have sponsors," she said arrogantly. "That is, those who can't do otherwise."

"Sponsors?" Heather repeated.

"Yes, it's free advertising for department stores and other businesses."

"Of course, Ashley doesn't require a sponsor," her stuck-up mother added quickly.

"It shows." Heather grinned and walked away.

The teenager peeked at the various models' clothes racks out of curiosity. To her surprise, several outfits carrying the exclusive "Jean-Paul" label hung on one. Just then Laura LaMonica ran up to her dressing table to get a lipstick.

"Excuse me," Heather said, pointing to the metal stand. "Are these your clothes?"

"Yes," she said nervously.

"Is Jean-Paul your sponsor?"

The model regarded her oddly. "Why?"

"Oh, I'm learning how contestants afford these wonderful wardrobes," Heather said casually.

"Well, Jean-Paul isn't my sponsor," Laura answered abruptly. Then she popped the lipstick into her handbag and hurried away.

She seems to be hiding something, Heather considered silently.

Then the teenage detective saw an even more amazing sight at Courtney Lewis's dress rack—it was loaded with Jean-Paul's designs! Heather shuffled through it and discovered Courtney had no other brands.

These clothes are worth as much as some houses, she estimated. *Even though the Lewises seem to have money, do they have that much?* Heather doubted it.

The teenager slowly became aware of the strong scent of perfume. It seemed familiar, but she couldn't place it. The contestants all used perfume, and the fragrances seemed to blend in the open dressing areas.

Just then a woman's husky voice jolted her. "What do you want?" the voice demanded.

The startled teenager swung around and found herself face-to-face with Mrs. Lewis. "Uh, nothing," she said stupidly.

The contestant's mother lunged at her, but Heather stepped out of the way in time to avoid being struck.

"You owe me an explanation!" Mrs. Lewis said furiously.

She regarded the woman's dagger-like nails. *I'd better be careful,* Heather decided.

"I'm working on my story for *Star Struck,*" she said innocently.

"Work on it someplace else!" Mrs. Lewis grabbed her arm.

"Ow!" Heather cried out. "Let go!" The woman's nails felt like a squadron of attacking mosquitos.

Instead she propelled the girl past staring models and out the dressing room door. Then she huffed back inside.

Heather rubbed her aching arm. *Great! Another bruise from this competition,* she thought unhappily.

"I've been looking for you!" Eric called out. Then he noticed something was wrong. "What happened?"

"Courtney Lewis's mother got rough with me," she remarked.

"Not everyone appreciates us," Eric soothed.

Heather was able to relax and think during the center city photo session. Outside Independence Hall the sound of neighing horses seized her attention. Heather watched Steven Ramsey shoo away bystanders, then spirit the models and escorts into old-fashioned carriages.

Brian and Joe climbed into one with Ashley Pitman and Laura LaMonica. But just as the driver pulled out of the loading zone, firecrackers exploded near the animals. Screams rang out as the coach's horse burst fearfully into the heavy traffic of the street.

Heather stared in shock at the nightmarish scene. Other horses reared up but didn't go onto the road. A mounted policeman galloped after the terrified horse as Eric enthusiastically snapped photo after photo. Then another officer moved his squad car into the traffic to divert it from the carriage. Moments later the coachman brought his horse and carriage to a stop.

The teenage reporter saw Brian and Joe get out unhurt. They were followed by a sobbing Laura and an enraged Ashley.

"Okay, who's responsible?" she shouted. "I'm tired of this garbage!" She stormed up to Steven Ramsey. "If you don't get this show on a safer road, I'll sue Pep Shampoo for all it's worth. Got it?" She poked his chest to drive home the point.

"Are you okay, Brian?" Heather asked.

"I think so." He smoothed back his wind-blown dark hair. "That was some ride."

Reporters and photographers swarmed around them with Eric in the lead.

"Hey, Laura!" one yelled. "What was that like?"

"Scary," the girl said, trying to look poised.

"Did your life flash before you?" the woman asked.

"Uh, you might say that," she smiled nervously.

Brian and Joe guided her away from the mob, and soon the vans took everyone back to the Music Fair. The incident had cast another long shadow across the competition.

Heather, Brian, and Joe went home for the afternoon. Heather went to her room to take a nap but lay wide awake replaying the carriage episode in her mind. This attack hadn't followed the usual pattern. Since all the contestants had been in horse-drawn carriages, any one of them could have been hurt, not just Kirsten or Ashley. *It strikes me as a copy cat crime,* she thought. *Unless it's worse than I thought, and all the models are in danger. I've got to get to the bottom of this!*

That evening a large crowd and a horde of journalists packed the Music Fair for the finals. The negative publicity had created a sensation.

Heather and Eric were coordinating their duties when a terrible scream came from the contestants' dressing area. The teenage reporter dropped everything and burst into the room. Other female reporters were on her heels.

What now? Heather wondered.

Then she saw what had happened. Ashley Pitman stood in front of her mirror shrieking at the top of her lungs. Her hair was purple!

11

Shocking Discoveries

W here is that Winchell woman?" Mrs. Pitman clenched her fists.

"Right here," Kirsten Neff pointed at the woman.

As Steven Ramsey's assistant approached the hysterical Pitmans, Kirsten caught Heather's eye and grinned. Ashley's crisis was somewhat amusing!

Although Joan Winchell looked startled by Ashley's purple hair, she responded defensively to Mrs. Pitman's demanding tone of voice. "What do you want?"

"What do you think I want?" Ashley mimicked sarcastically. "You did this!" She shoved a lock of purple hair toward the woman's face.

"That's crazy!" Joan exclaimed. "How can I be responsible?"

"Because," Ashley steamed, "you supply us with Pep Shampoo." She spit out the last two words. "You deliberately put something in mine to ruin my hair for tonight. Admit it."

Female reporters now flooded the dressing room, which grew warmer by the minute. "Get those cameras out of her face!" Mrs. Pitman stormed, pushing photographers away. When they refused, Ashley hastily wrapped a towel around her head.

"I didn't do it," Joan Winchell spat.

Ashley didn't hurl another accusation. Instead she threw a fist, catching the coordinator's assistant on the chin. The startled woman staggered backward. Then a policewoman appeared, stepping between them.

"She attacked me!" Joan Winchell charged, rubbing her chin.

Ashley screeched, "I had every right to hit you! You're trying to prevent me from winning. Admit it!"

"Hold on!" Officer Florence Crane asserted. Then she asked Joan Winchell, "Do you want to press charges?"

Tension mounted in the room. For the first time since the troubled modeling contest began, Ashley looked scared. If Joan Winchell took legal action, the brunette would be disqualified. The two women's eyes met and locked for several tense seconds.

"No, I won't," she finally decided. "And not because I'm such a nice guy either," she quickly added. Staring at the model, she mocked, "I want to see you get out of this one, Ashley."

The young woman's eyes blazed, but she controlled her temper as her mother led her away.

"Where are you going?" eager reporters questioned. In response, the Pitmans shoved them aside.

Excited conversations filled the dressing room. The other models tensely asked each other what ghastly thing might happen next.

Heather went over to Kirsten. "How are you?" she asked sincerely, hugging the young woman.

"Much better," the blonde smiled. "I'm still a little weak, but I'll make it tonight." She gave a little laugh. "As funny as it seemed, I do feel badly for Ashley."

A reporter noticed Kirsten and came over. "I see you made it back," the woman said. "Are you up to tonight?" Others followed, nudging Heather out of the way. After a few minutes, the teenager saw Laura LaMonica sitting by herself and walked over to her.

"How's it going?" Heather asked.

"Okay," she smiled stiffly. Laura seemed afraid of Heather.

"Could I ask you something? This isn't part of an interview," the young journalist added quickly.

"I guess." She sounded hesitant.

"Who's your sponsor for the contest?" Heather inquired.

Laura's eyes darted about the room nervously. "Why?"

"I'd like to know what's going on around here," Heather explained.

The model became upset. "You don't think I'd hurt anyone?"

"Of course not," the teenager assured her. "But someone is, and they need to be stopped."

Laura ran a hand through her thick, dark brown hair, and it snapped right back into shape. "I didn't have a sponsor when I came. I bought my stuff with money I earned last summer when I was home from college." She hesitated for a moment. "When I got here the other day, Jean-Paul started hanging around. He said I'd have a great shot at winning the contest if I wore his fashions and talked me into taking some outfits." She quickly added, "He said there were no rules against it." Then she sighed loudly. "He also said if I won, he'd make me the highest paid model in the world."

"That's a big promise," Heather remarked.

"One he obviously doesn't intend to keep," Laura added bitterly.

"What do you mean?" the girl frowned.

"Since he and Courtney Lewis's mother became chummy, he won't even speak to me!" Laura exclaimed.

That explains all the Jean-Paul designs on Courtney's rack! Heather thought excitedly.

She was about to ask Laura another question, but Joan Winchell chased the newswomen out of the dressing room.

A few minutes later Heather walked slowly toward the circular theater, deep in thought. *Could Mrs. Lewis be the woman I overheard at Tenley's yesterday?* the teenager wondered. Suddenly she snapped her fingers. *It was her! When she grabbed me today, I smelled her strong perfume, the same one I picked up at Tenley's!*

Although Heather wanted to pursue the clue, the sound of troubled voices coming from Marci's suite caused her to stop and listen. *That sounds like Steven Ramsey and Joan Winchell with Marci,* Heather thought. The conversation became increasingly heated.

"There's no love between the two of you—or you and Pep Shampoo," Marci accused. "You and Steven have every reason to undermine this contest."

"I did not put purple dye in Ashley's shampoo!" Joan defended.

It's so frustrating to have more than one person with strong motives! Heather complained silently.

Steven Ramsey's booming voice came through the closed door. "I resent that deeply! I may have problems with Pep's directors, but only a twisted person would hurt those girls. Nor would I pick an assistant capable of harming them."

Maybe I can rule them out, Heather judged.

Suddenly Eric called out to her. "Heather! I got some great shots of Ashley running out of here with her purple hair!"

The teenager waved her hands frantically for him to be quiet.

"What gives?" he asked softly, not one to give away a scoop.

She explained quickly in a low voice, then told him to listen.

"Those girls don't trust me now," complained Joan Winchell. "What will we do?"

Steven responded, "I'll need you to take over, Marci."

"Why me?" she shouted. "I have my own duties."

"You only have to look good and provide a little TV commentary. And then Luke shares that job," he stated unsympathetically.

"He'll get more air time if I do this!" she pouted.

"May I remind you that for the duration of this contest, I am your supervisor, Marci?" Steven pulled rank.

Then there was silence. Eric nearly squooshed Heather in his attempt to hear what was happening inside.

"Give me some breathing room!" she whispered.

Then they heard, "At least I can have my assistant help," Marci said peevishly. "Where is that girl anyway?" She sounded impatient.

Steven responded, "She has a name—Jenn McLaughlin. Use it. And furthermore, you are not to take your wrath out on her. Is that clear, Marci?"

"Perfectly," she said. Even from a distance Heather and Eric could hear her teeth clench. "Oh, Jenn!" she called in a voice dripping with false pleasantness.

The next thing they knew, Marci led Jenn out the door. Heather and Eric backed off just in time. To the *Star Struck* journalists' surprise, a horde of other newspeople suddenly descended on Marci.

"This is getting out of hand," Heather heard a familiar voice say. She spotted Chloé St. Johns at a close distance and hurried over to her.

"Did you mean the threats or the press?" Heather asked, tongue in cheek.

The tall woman smiled. "Both."

Then Heather took her out one of the back exits. She explained that Jean-Paul had given clothes to Courtney and to Laura LaMonica.

"I am not surprised," Chloé stated.

Heather had an inspiration. "Have you ever seen his handwriting?" she asked.

"Not for years. Why do you ask?" the ex-model tilted her head.

"On my first day here, I saw Ashley's warning note. The handwriting was thick and heavy," she explained. "I remember thinking it was foolish to leave such an obvious clue."

"That could easily be his writing," she said. "It is distinctive, as I recall. And," Chloé added, "he is arrogant enough to think he will not be caught in his deceptions. I must go now," she said, checking the time. "The show is about to begin."

To the amazement of everyone in the contest, selecting the finalists went smoothly. Even Ashley, sporting a wig from a hair salon, landed one of the ten spots. Kirsten, Laura LaMonica, Courtney Lewis, and six other young women also advanced to the last round. Afterward, several losers eagerly packed their things and fled the tension.

Heather scrambled to interview the models she had not previously met, and Eric took their pictures. After completing her work, the teenage reporter looked for Kirsten and asked to speak privately with her. She wanted to find out who had food poisoned her.

"I heard that you ate what everyone else did before you got sick yesterday. What about the day before? Usually food poisoning takes a day or so to kick in."

"I did then, too," she reflected.

"You can't remember anything different?"

"No, not really," she said.

"Did you always serve yourself?" Heather pursued.

"No," she responded, "At lunch yesterday someone brought my sandwich to me. Normally there's a big tray, and we fix our own. But we were too busy getting ready for the show at the mall."

"Who was it?" Heather asked.

Kirsten's answer astonished her. "Your friend, Jenn."

"Jenn!" The teenager felt light-headed. "She works for Marci and Luke."

"As I said, yesterday everyone was rushing around. She just pitched in and helped."

"We can rule her out as a suspect," Heather said firmly, "but she may know where the food came from."

"That's enough for now," Kirsten's aunt announced, walking up to the young women. "You've had a big day."

"Yes, you have," Heather smiled. "And tomorrow's even bigger!"

Kirsten groaned. "Don't remind me. I'm so nervous."

Heather went off to a quiet corner of the press room to sort through all the clues she'd picked up so far. She jotted down some notes until her pen ran out of ink. The teenager rummaged through her pack looking for another pen, but didn't find one. Then she spotted Eric's camera bag. Heather opened the outside flap and reached inside. Her fingers closed around a strange object. When she pulled it out, Heather caught her breath—a string of firecrackers!

12

Reckless Endangerment

The sound of Eric's voice startled the teenager.

"I'm glad that's done," he said brightly. But then his face clouded when he saw Heather's expression. "What's wrong?"

"That's what I'm wondering about you," she countered.

Eric chuckled nervously. "What do you mean?"

"This." She tossed the firecrackers at him.

Now he grew angry. "What were you doing going through my stuff?"

"I needed a pen," she said indignantly. "You almost killed people!"

"No one was going to get killed," he scoffed, kicking a foot at the air.

"You took a foolish chance," Heather accused, hands on hips. "Did you also knock me down in the parking lot, slash Chloé's tires, food poison Kirsten, and turn Ashley's hair purple?"

Although she still believed Jean-Paul was the master-mind, Heather realized Eric might have been partners with him and Mrs. Lewis.

"I didn't do any of those things," he insisted. Then he became sober. "And I didn't mean to hurt anyone."

Heather tended to believe the photographer, but she was still angry. "Then why did you do it?"

Eric shoved his hands in his pockets and looked down. "I wanted to get some good pictures."

"Pictures!" she exploded. "That is the most selfish thing I've heard in a long time—even here. I can't be-lieve you risked peoples' lives for some stupid pictures!"

Other reporters gathered around them as Heather turned from him in disgust.

"Where are you going?" he asked, blocking her way.

"To make a phone call," she responded.

But Eric wouldn't let her get by. He put his hands on her shoulders and pleaded with her not to tell anyone. He abruptly backed away when he spotted Brian and Joe, who had come to take Heather home.

"What's the problem?" her brother asked.

"Brian, would you please keep an eye on Eric? I need to call our editor to find out what to do with him," Heather stormed. "He threw those firecrackers at Inde-pendence Hall today!"

The college freshmen moved menacingly toward Eric. Heather knew they wouldn't hit him, but she did hope they'd make him sweat. Then she called Rhonda Cowley and told her about the incident. The editor asked to speak directly to the young man.

"She wants to talk to you." Heather handed him the receiver. "And is she ever mad!"

Eric gulped and took the phone. He said only a few words, then gave it back to Heather. "Ms. Cowley?" she asked. "What happened?"

"I fired him, that's what!" the editor retorted. "I encourage enthusiasm, not criminal behavior. The only problem is, what to do about pictures?" She paused. "Are you any good?"

"Me?" Heather rolled a strand of hair around her forefinger. "I'm an average . . . Oh, wait a minute!" She motioned to Joe, a Kirby College yearbook photographer. Heather asked whether he'd help if she took the assignment. She needed as much time as possible to solve the mystery.

"Of course I will," Joe said, eager to help.

When she hung up a few minutes later, Heather noticed Brian and Eric weren't in the press room.

"He took Eric to the security office," Joe explained.

"What a rotten thing to do!" she exclaimed.

"He deserved it, Heather."

"Uh, I meant to say what a rotten thing for Eric to do!" she clarified.

"You solved the mystery!" Joe smiled joyfully.

But Heather shook her head. "Eric did a stupid thing, but he's no villain. I have others in mind."

"Okay," Joe said slowly. "Want to tell me about it?"

"Not just yet," the pretty teenager smiled.

He shrugged. "I'm going to wait outside." Then he added, "Will you get Jenn?"

"After I finish here," Heather promised. "Then we'll be right with you."

"See you out front," he said with a wave.

Heather faxed her stories, then talked to Chloé St. Johns and a few other journalists about Eric. Then she took Chloé aside.

"I'm afraid Jean-Paul is planning something really awful for the last day," she said.

Chloé did not try to reassure her. "He may. That man will stop at nothing to satisfy his ego." Her eyes narrowed. "Be careful Heather."

"I will," she said. "By the way, Chloé, have you seen Jenn McLaughlin?"

She laughed. "Yes, the poor darling is running around as Marci Bentley barks instructions at her. I am sure she will welcome her bed tonight."

"I'm sure she will," Heather laughed. "See you tomorrow!"

The teenager found her best friend crying in the dressing room. Heather sat next to her on the bench and put her arm around Jenn. "You're worn out, aren't you?"

"Marci and Luke are tyrants, but it's not just that." The redhead dabbed at her eyes and blew her nose. "I think Kirsten Neff got sick because of me. She didn't even look at me tonight."

This was exactly what Heather wanted to discuss with Jenn! "What makes you think that?" she asked.

"Because I gave her a sandwich right before we left for the mall yesterday," she explained.

"Are you sure that's what made her sick?" Heather asked.

"I think so," Jenn said. "She seemed fine until she ate it."

"Who organizes meals?" asked the young detective.

"Joan Winchell gives the orders to a caterer. But yesterday she was so busy she borrowed me from Marci and Luke to help with lunch."

The thought crossed Heather's mind that Joan might have set Jenn up to take the blame. But from what she had observed, Heather didn't believe Steven Ramsey or his assistant would harm others to get back at Pep Shampoo.

"Jenn," she inquired, "does the caterer know what food goes to each model?"

"Uh huh. They have a list of the contestants' names and what food they want. You know that big table with a grid?"

"The one with a square for each contestant?" Heather asked.

Jenn nodded. "Yesterday the caterer put each model's food in a paper sack with her name. Then I matched them to the squares."

Heather pursed her lips. "Isn't that where the toiletries Pep Shampoo supplies go?"

"Yes. That's what the table's really for," Jenn said.

"So someone could have easily put purple dye in Ashley's shampoo," Heather concluded.

"Uh huh. Getting back to lunch yesterday—after I had put the lunch bags on each square, Joan asked me to deliver the lunches instead. The models and their moms were real busy getting ready for the fashion show." Jenn's blue eyes held more hope than tears now. She sensed her best friend could clear her.

"So there were times when the food was out of your sight?" Heather inquired.

Jenn started to shake her head, then remembered something. "Come to think of it, Marci called me away for a few minutes to help her find a sweater."

"What happened when you returned?" Heather was growing excited.

"It doesn't seem like a big deal . . . " Jenn hesitated.

"What?" Heather demanded. "It could be important."

"Well, I found a model's mother hovering around the sandwiches. When I asked how I could help, she seemed unnerved. Then she complained I was making everyone wait too long for lunch."

"Who's mother was it?" Heather asked, sparks of excitement flashing in her eyes.

When Jenn had to think a moment, Heather could hardly control her impatience. Finally her friend remembered. "It was Courtney Lewis's mom."

Bingo! Heather thought. *She's the mother of the girl with a fortune in clothes by Jean-Paul and who screamed at me when I found them. I'll bet she engineered the purple dye incident, too.*

"Knock, knock," Jenn interrupted. "What's going on up there?" She pointed to Heather's head.

"I'll explain everything on the way home," she said quickly. "But don't worry. You didn't food poison Kirsten."

"Thank God!" she sighed.

As they started to leave for the night, the policewoman she'd seen before intercepted Heather to question her about Eric.

"I'll meet you outside," Jenn said, walking away.

"Joe's waiting out there," Heather called after her.

The sixteen-year-old went with Officer Crane to the security area where Brian told her another police officer had taken Eric to the station.

"He'll probably post bail until a trial—unless he pleads guilty now to reckless endangerment," Crane added.

"What sort of penalty does that carry?" Heather asked.

"Oh, usually a fine or community service while the guy's on probation," the policewoman explained.

Heather wanted to discuss some other things as well, including the rollerblading and tire slashing incidents.

"We picked up a kid wandering around the parking lot this afternoon," Officer Straiter, Crane's partner, offered. "He looked like he was up to something."

"What happened?" Heather asked breathlessly.

"At first he claimed he'd done nothing wrong. Then he finally admitted someone paid him to knock you and your friend down and slash Ms. St. Johns' tires."

"Who is that someone?" Heather asked.

"The youngster doesn't know," the policeman said. "He only got notes with instructions and money."

"How did he get the notes?" Heather asked.

"Through the caterer's helper," Officer Crane responded.

"Do you have any of those notes?" Heather was beside herself, certain they had come from Jean-Paul.

"Not really. But the caterer's helper had this," Straiter handed her a piece of paper from a folder.

Heather's heart raced. The writing was heavy and thick!

13

Jenn Disappears

The message read, "No mayonnaise."

Heather clapped her hands together. "This has to be Jean-Paul's writing," she announced.

The teenager quickly told the police how it matched Kirsten and Ashley's notes. "I'm sure they're from Jean-Paul," she added, "because an American wouldn't say, 'No mayonnaise.' He'd say, 'Hold the mayo,' or 'No mayo.'"

The officers and her brother regarded her with admiration.

"You might just have something there," Crane commented.

Heather handed the note back to Straiter. "I'd feel a lot calmer if I knew you were watching Jean-Paul closely. He's no doubt got something even worse in mind for the grand finale."

The policewoman was puzzled. "Why would he do these things? He's got nothing to gain by it."

"He seems to think so," Brian shrugged.

"Don't worry; we already have plans in place for extra security tomorrow," Officer Straiter promised. "But thank you for sharing your thoughts and observations."

Brian and Heather found Joe outside. They told him what was happening with Eric, and also the news about the rollerblader.

"I can't wait to call Chloé!" Heather said. But then she frowned. "Where's Jenn?"

"I thought she was with you," Joe answered.

"She was until the police questioned me. Jenn said she was on her way outside." Heather sighed. "I'll bet Marci found a last-minute thing for her to do. You guys wait here while I go find her."

But Marci and Luke's suites were both empty. Only Steven Ramsey and Joan Winchell were around, answering a reporter's questions about the troubled contest.

Heather cleared her throat. "Excuse me, Mr. Ramsey, but have you seen Jenn McLaughlin?"

He became irritated. "No, why should I?"

"She was supposed to meet us outside. I thought maybe you found extra work for her," Heather explained.

"Did you check the dressing room?" Joan Winchell suggested.

"Yes, but she's not there!" The teenager was growing concerned.

"Another bizarre incident?" the reporter asked.

"Mr. Ramsey, I know you're busy, but could I please speak with you privately?" Heather requested.

He excused himself and followed the teenager to a more private spot. Heather told him what she and Jenn had figured out right before they separated—that Kirsten Neff had been deliberately food poisoned.

"That's horrible!" he stated, wringing his hands. "Wait here for me. I'll get rid of that reporter and close the building."

"Please bring Brian and Joe back here," she asked.

Ten minutes later Steven Ramsey, Joan Winchell, Heather, Brian, and Joe combed the Music Fair for Jenn. When they came up empty, Ramsey summoned Officers Straiter and Crane to join the search. But Jenn was nowhere to be found. Sighing heavily, Ramsey concluded, "We'd better call Jenn's parents."

Officer Straiter interrupted. "Don't worry about that—we'll do it."

He and his partner followed Jenn's glum friends back to Kirby. When Mrs. McLaughlin answered the door, she looked frightened by the sight of Philadelphia police officers. She ushered the group into the formal living room.

"What's wrong? Where's Jenn?" Her voice rose, and she seemed on the verge of hysteria.

"Is your husband at home?" Officer Straiter asked.

"Yes," Mrs. McLaughlin said. "Heather, please go upstairs and get him."

The teenager obediently raced up the steps and found Jenn's dad rummaging through the hall closet and mumbling in frustration. Otherwise the house was silent, and she assumed Jenn's little brothers were asleep.

"Heather!" he jumped up when he saw her standing there. "You surprised me!"

"Mrs. McLaughlin wants you to come downstairs," she said gently.

He dropped the items he held and raced ahead, sensing something was wrong. The officers introduced themselves, then told Jenn's parents what had happened.

"I knew we shouldn't have let her get involved with those people!" Mrs. McLaughlin sobbed.

Then the doorbell rang. It was Heather and Brian's parents. Brian had called them to let them know what was going on. Mr. and Mrs. Reed were distressed by the news and had come to see if there was anything they could do.

The officers asked a few questions, obtained a picture of Jenn, and then excused themselves to continue the search.

"I have a strong feeling this is going to work out fine," Straiter smiled reassuringly.

Heather showed them outside. "Please try to find Jean-Paul and Mrs. Lewis," she requested. "I'm sure they're behind this."

After the officers left, the McLaughlins and their friends prayed together for Jenn's safety.

Heather slept poorly that night. She tossed on her bed through the long, dark hours trying to figure out what had happened to her friend. Though she felt strongly that Jean-Paul and Mrs. Lewis were somehow responsible, she didn't know how or why.

Early the next morning she got out the list showing the finalists' names and their hotels. Heather's first call was to Courtney Lewis.

"I'm sorry to hear about Jenn," the model said. "But I don't know anything that could help you."

Suddenly her mother yanked the phone away and sputtered, "Who do you think you are, waking up my daughter? You media people need to learn a little respect. If you bother my daughter again, you'll be sorry." With that she slammed down the receiver.

Heather stared angrily at the phone. "I wish I could get Courtney alone!" she said aloud. Then she thought, *I'd like to know how close her mother is to Jean-Paul.*

The sixteen-year-old phoned the other models, but all had left the theater-in-the-round long before Heather had last seen Jenn. Still, they expressed concern about Jenn's disappearance—that is, all except Ashley Pitman.

"I don't pay attention to the help," Ashley had retorted.

Heather felt frustrated, not only by the lack of information she'd gathered, but because the police had not yet questioned any of the models.

Before she, Brian, and Joe left for rehearsals at the Music Fair, Mrs. Reed told Heather sternly, "I expect you to be careful. No heroics."

She never knew what to expect from her precocious teenager, and that sometimes created tension between them.

"I'll be fine," Heather pledged. But her mother wasn't convinced.

Mrs. Reed's voice caught. "If anything should happen to you . . . " She hugged her daughter tightly.

"Don't worry, we'll take care of her," Joe said seriously.

But both Brian and Mrs. Reed knew better. When Heather got something in her mind, there was no stopping her.

On the way to the Music Fair, Heather did ask Joe for a favor. "On top of writing stories and looking for Jenn, I may not be able to take many pictures this morning. I only need a few of the contestants as they go through the last day." She paused. "Will you do it?"

"I'd be happy to," he said kindly, taking Heather's camera.

At the theater-in-the-round, several reporters asked Heather, Brian, and Joe about Jenn's disappearance. The trio answered the basic questions, but they gave few details. Mr. Reed had cautioned them on this earlier because he didn't want anything they said to jeopardize Jenn's welfare.

A troubled Chloé St. Johns took Heather aside. "I have a terrible feeling about this," she whispered. "I think Jenn gained information she should not have had." She frowned. "But Heather, Jean-Paul was not here when Jenn vanished."

"Not here?" Heather repeated. "Where was he?"

"He left right after the finalists were named. He only gave one interview," Chloé said.

"What kind of mood was he in?" the teenager asked, eagerly searching for any clue that could lead her to Jenn.

"He was anxious to leave."

"Is he here this morning?"

Chloé shook her head. "No, but the judges are not due until early this evening. I am here now to cover Jenn's disappearance. This has become a major news story."

Heather saw her brother and Joe walk toward her with Officers Crane and Straiter. Unfortunately they still hadn't found Jenn.

"An all-night search party found no trace of her," Crane said. Seeing their concern, she added, "Don't lose hope. I'm sure we'll find her."

Heather wasn't so sure.

She went back to the dressing area where the finalists tensely asked about Jenn. A willowy blonde named Dawn Schneider cried, "I don't know what will go wrong next! I'm sorry I ever entered this rotten contest!"

Ashley Pitman clucked at her in disgust. "The job probably got too hard for Jenn," she said coldly. "That's my opinion."

"Your opinion doesn't count for much!" Courtney Lewis shouted. "You're so conceited, Ashley. You can't think about anybody but yourself!"

"I'll second that!" Laura LaMonica added.

Heather had felt like slapping Ashley, but the other contestants' remarks took the urge away. Besides, another fight was the last thing anyone needed. Happily, though, it was a good time to talk to Courtney because her mother wasn't around.

"Courtney, could I please talk to you?" she asked.

"Do you think you should?" she asked uneasily.

That only heightened the young detective's interest. "Yes, I do," she replied.

Blonde-haired Courtney sighed. "All right. But please make it short."

Heather did. She asked directly, "Is Jean-Paul your sponsor?"

"Um, not exactly," she said, scrunching her well-defined eyebrows. "Are you referring to the clothes I have?" Heather nodded. "My mother bought them for me."

"Those are pretty expensive clothes," Heather commented.

"Yes, I know," Courtney agreed tensely. "Are you implying that my mother wants me to wear Jean-Paul clothes so he'll favor me?" she asked in complete innocence.

Heather didn't have an opportunity to answer. An angry voice and a shove interrupted the conversation.

"I told you not to bother my daughter!" Mrs. Lewis said sharply. "She is not to speak to the press until after the competition." Her eyes bored into the teenager.

Courtney gave Heather an apologetic look.

Although Heather wanted to demand an explanation for Jenn's disappearance, believing Mrs. Lewis may have been involved, the teenage reporter forced herself to stay calm. "I'll be going then," she said. Turning to Courtney she remarked sincerely, "I hope you do well tonight."

"Do well?" Mrs. Lewis mimicked. "Do well? Courtney is going to win!"

14

Time Runs Out

Heather walked outside into the beautiful spring morning. She was so worried about Jenn, she needed to clear her thoughts. Heather strongly suspected Mrs. Lewis and Jean-Paul of making an illegal arrangement to secure Courtney's victory. But she lacked hard evidence and had no idea what they had planned.

They're so crafty! she sighed.

Just then Heather spotted a tall, muscular man head toward the back of the Music Fair. He kept looking around as if to make sure no one was watching.

What's he doing? the teenager pondered. *I'll shadow him at a distance.*

She saw the man slip behind two large run-down truck trailers. *What are those for?* she wondered. They seemed out of place.

In that moment of reflection, Heather lost sight of the man and hurried to the trailers to catch up. However, she found only an eerie silence.

I don't like this, she thought. *I can't see him, but he might be able to see me.*

And she was right. Just then she was hit from behind and knocked to her knees!

"What's going on?" she demanded, trying to turn around.

Her answer was a blow to the back of her head.

When Heather woke up, she found herself chained to something and lying on an old mattress. She gave a start when her eyes focused on someone—or something—sitting next to her in the semi-darkness!

"Who are you?" Heather whispered. She still felt groggy from the thump on the head.

"You're awake!" a familiar voice shouted.

"Jenn?" she squinted. "Is that you?"

"Yes, it's me!" her friend answered with an awkward hug.

"Are you all right?" Heather asked. "I've been so worried about you!"

"I'm okay." Jenn smoothed Heather's long hair away from her eyes. "Don't try to sit up. It feels like you had a pretty hard blow to the head."

Though Heather couldn't see, Jenn was a mess too. She hadn't taken a bath or brushed her hair since the day before.

"Did anyone hurt you?" Heather asked.

"Shake me up? Yes. Hurt me? No."

Heather felt dazed. "Are we in a trailer behind the Music Fair?"

"I'm not real sure," Jenn admitted. "They brought me here a few hours ago, and I was blindfolded."

"They?" Heather started to sit up.

"Don't do that," Jenn warned. "Try to relax." Although she wanted to tell her friend everything, she didn't think Heather was ready yet. "I'll tell you everything after you've rested."

"Jenn?" the teenager mumbled.

"Yes?" she asked.

"Are we alone?"

"Uh huh. Now please rest."

Heather fell right back to sleep, content that Jenn was alive and well. She awakened what seemed like hours later.

"This wouldn't be a five-star hotel, would it?" she asked dryly. She obviously felt better.

Jenn smiled. "No, it's not. The food isn't too hot either," she said, handing her a loaf of plain white bread and a box of juice. "Here's lunch."

"Lunch? What time is it?" Heather yawned.

Jenn strained to see her watch in the dim light. "Quarter after twelve."

Heather accepted her share of bread and ate hungrily as she thought about where she was and how she had gotten there. Jenn seemed relieved.

"Am I ever glad you found me!" she stated. "I was pretty scared for a while."

"I haven't exactly come with the cavalry," Heather rattled her chains. They were attached to a bar that ran along the wall.

"No, but you'll figure something out. You always do," Jenn said confidently.

"So how and when did you get here?" her petite friend asked.

"Well, last night I was on my way to meet you and the guys when I remembered Marci had asked me to turn all the lights out in the dressing room."

"Then what?" Heather asked with her mouth full.

"I overheard a man and woman talking, and it didn't seem right. Sort of like what happened to you at the mall. So I hid behind a pillar and listened—like you. The woman told the guy he'd get five thousand dollars when he 'did the job.'"

"What job?" Heather paused in mid bite.

"You won't believe this," Jenn said. She paused dramatically, then continued, "Kidnapping Ashley Pitman's mother!"

Heather was astonished. "Why?"

"Because none of the threats worked."

"The woman was Mrs. Lewis. Right?"

"How did you know?" Jenn cried out.

Heather told her redhead friend everything she'd missed. Then Jenn continued her story.

"I heard Mrs. Lewis say it was her last resort," she explained. "She figured if Mrs. Pitman were missing, Ashley wouldn't have the will to go through with the contest."

"And you must have been caught listening," Heather expressed.

Jenn groaned. "I hiccupped, and they grabbed me before I could get away."

"Is the guy I followed back here the same one you found with Mrs. Lewis?"

"Uh huh."

"Who is he?"

"I don't know," Jenn responded, "but I think he's been around the Music Fair."

"Hmm," Heather reflected. She couldn't decide how he had fit in before now. "What else do you know?" She tried to sit comfortably on the aged mattress.

"Well, Mrs. Lewis tried to bump Kirsten from the competition with that food poisoning. Now she doesn't think Kirsten will win because she is still weak and probably won't make a good impression on the judges."

"She must have contaminated Kirsten's sandwich right before you found her hanging around the table!" Heather stated.

"Yes." She sighed. "I feel terrible about not preventing it."

Heather put a hand on Jenn's arm. "I'm sure you do, but you didn't know what she was up to."

"True," Jenn said feeling somewhat better. Then she continued her story. "Mrs. Lewis also considered doing something to Laura LaMonica. But then she told her accomplice she didn't want to take that many chances."

Heather shifted again. It was impossible to get comfortable with her right leg chained. *And what is Jean-Paul's part in this nasty plot?* she wondered.

"We have to get out of here so we can warn the police," she told Jenn.

"But how?" she fretted.

Heather didn't answer right away. She strongly suspected Mrs. Lewis would try to get rid of all of them. Otherwise they could testify against her. The sound of a train outside filled their compartment for a minute, and the teenager perked up. "We are in those old trailers! The Music Fair must use them for storage."

"How do you know?" Jenn inquired.

"Because that's the commuter train than runs past." She thought silently for a few moments then asked, "Do you know what they are planning to do to Mrs. Pitman?"

Jenn said, "Not really. I don't think they actually intended to seriously hurt anyone at first. But things have gotten out of hand. Mrs. Lewis is crazy. I'm really scared, Heather. When I got caught, she looked like she was ready to do me in right then and there." Jenn shuddered from the terrible memory. "But that guy warned her not to ruin everything."

"You said they didn't bring you here right away?"

"Uh huh. They blindfolded me and took me to a motel," Jenn said. "This morning, the guy brought me here."

"And nobody saw you?" Heather marveled. "You'd look pretty obvious in a blindfold."

"They put me in the back of a van."

"Poor girl!" Heather sympathized.

Then she thought for a long while about how they could escape. She stood slowly and went as far as the chain allowed to see if there was a second door in the trailer. She also ran her hands along the wall for signs of structural weaknesses. If she found them, Heather and Jenn might be able to apply enough pressure to make the wall give out. Her lack of success discouraged her, and the girls sat quietly for several minutes.

Suddenly Jenn clapped the palm of her hand to her forehead. "That's it!"

"What?" Heather sat up straighter.

"I just remembered where I've seen our kidnapper before! He's the caterer's assistant!" she shouted.

Just then the lock on the door rattled. Moments later the sound of squeaking hinges and the smell of Chantal perfume filled the musty trailer.

Heather's pulse raced.

"Move!" Courtney's mother ordered hoarsely. "And quit dragging your feet or you won't get your shoes back at all." She shoved someone down on the crowded, dirty mattress, knocking Jenn into Heather. They toppled over like dominos, and the impact made Heather's head ache again.

"You're so clever, trying to make noise with those high heels," Mrs. Lewis mocked. Her peal of laughter sent shivers down the girls' spines. "No one can hear you now! I'll be back right after the rehearsal," she snarled.

"If you have any sins to confess, now would be a good time."

She laughed again wickedly and locked the heavy door behind her. There seemed no way out!

15

Rescue!

Mrs. Pitman, red-faced from her struggle, was more acid-tongued than usual.

"You!" she exclaimed when she saw Heather. The teenager couldn't tell if that was good or bad. Then the older woman squinted at Jenn in the murky light. "Aren't you Miss Bentley's servant?" She frowned at Jenn's disordered appearance. "You don't look like much."

The girl's blue eyes narrowed. Then almost with a laugh she said, "Mrs. Pitman, you wouldn't want to see yourself right now, either."

She was right. Ashley's mother looked like she'd been caught in a wind tunnel.

"What happened?" Heather asked as she undid the ropes tightly binding the woman's wrists. She had difficulty because the clasps on Mrs. Pitman's gold bracelets kept getting in the way.

"Should you free her?" Jenn worried. "Mrs. Lewis might not like it."

"I don't like this rope!" the woman retorted.

111

As Heather worked to untie the rope, Mrs. Pitman told them about her ordeal.

"This morning after driving Ashley to the Music Fair, I went to the mall to pick up my dress for tonight. In the parking lot a man came up to me and asked for a ride. He looked vaguely familiar, but I turned my back on him. Then he poked a gun at me and ordered me to drive to a dreadful neighborhood." She shuddered.

"Was he the guy who works for the caterer?" Jenn asked.

"That's him!" Mrs. Pitman exclaimed.

Heather finally got the rope untied, and it fell to the dirty floor. Mrs. Pitman opened and closed her hands to get the circulation moving.

"Anyway, the man blindfolded and tied me up, then had me lie across the back seat with a stadium blanket over me. Then that female creature met us here. She did not appreciate the fuss I made." Mrs. Pitman felt the runs in her pantyhose.

Suddenly the dignified woman shrieked and jumped up. "Did you see that bug? There are cockroaches in here," she said in horror. When she sat down again, Mrs. Pitman pulled her feet under her skirt.

"It's pretty gross, isn't it?" Heather agreed.

"I should say so," Ashley's mother retorted. "What is the meaning of this outrage?"

Heather told her about the plot to stop Ashley and Kirsten from defeating Courtney Lewis.

"When threats and 'accidents' failed, they decided to kidnap you until after the contest. They figured Ashley would be too upset to go on," she concluded.

"How dare they!" she stormed. After calming down, the woman asked, "How did you get caught up in this?"

"I've been investigating the mishaps undercover," Heather explained. "Unfortunately, Jenn overheard a conversation and ended up in here."

"Are you a policewoman?" Mrs. Pitman questioned.

Before Heather could answer, Jenn spoke up. "She's an amateur detective," she said proudly and explained other mysteries her friend had solved. After she finished, the three sat quietly for a while.

"I always thought Mrs. Lewis had something strange on her mind," Mrs. Pitman finally remarked. "And I know Jean-Paul's out for his own glory, but why is this other dreadful man involved?" She dragged out the word "dreadful" so it sounded exactly like what it meant.

"He's doing the dirty work," Heather offered.

"Isn't there some way out of this awful place?" Jenn asked.

"There must be, but I can't get very far with this chain," Heather said.

"Is escape possible?" the older woman fretted.

"All things are possible with God," Jenn smiled.

"Must we get religious?" Mrs. Pitman asked irritably. "It seems so gloomy."

The two teenagers giggled.

"Mrs. Pitman, you're the only one who can walk freely. Look around for weak spots we could push through," Heather directed.

"Who made you the boss?" she arched her eyebrows.

"No one. If you have other ideas, I'd welcome them," Heather said patiently.

"All right. But I'll only do it if you lend me your shoes. This floor is disgusting!"

Heather glanced at Mrs. Pitman's large feet. "Jenn's would fit better."

The redhead sighed as she reluctantly removed her shoes. They were also too small, but Mrs. Pitman shoved them on. Tight was better than barefoot.

As the woman examined the chamber she asked, "Are those horrid people going to hurt my Ashley?"

"No—but I'm not so sure about the three of us. We know too much," said Heather.

"Barbarians!" she remarked indignantly.

They searched desperately for a means of escape well into mid afternoon. But the trailer only grew stuffier and dustier from their effort. At one point Heather thought there might be a flimsy part of the ceiling. Then a rein-forced metal layer appeared when she bored through with the heel of her shoe. They all felt thirsty and dirty, not to mention angry and afraid.

"I'd give anything for a restroom," Mrs. Pitman sighed.

"Why don't we just scream at the tops of our lungs?" Jenn suggested out of total frustration.

The sound of footsteps on the stairs struck terror to each of their hearts. Was this it?

When the door opened, Mrs. Lewis asked, "And how are we?"

Her captives regarded her disdainfully in spite of their fear.

"You know, I only planned to detain Mrs. Pitman," she said innocently. "But you nosy girls fouled everything up. Now more permanent measures are called for." Her laughter sounded more like a witch's cackle. "Hurry, Carl!" she ordered her accomplice. "We need to get them out of here!"

He began unfastening the girls' chains.

"Just don't get any ideas," Mrs. Lewis warned, holding a small pistol. "Or maybe you'd prefer to die sooner?" she sneered.

Then the cruel woman swung the door open and helped Carl lead the trio outside. Jenn winced when her bare feet met piercing gravel; Mrs. Pitman had refused to give back the teenager's shoes.

Their abductors led them a few feet into some woods. Just beyond the line of trees was a sharp drop that ended in commuter train tracks.

"Take a good look, Miss Know-It-All." One of Mrs. Lewis's well-manicured hands shoved Heather toward the edge.

The girl's heart pounded as she stumbled in her heels. *It's a long way down!* she gulped. "God, please save us!" the teenager whispered.

Mrs. Lewis sniffed disapprovingly, then consulted her watch. "The next train will arrive any minute now."

Jenn squeezed Heather's hand. Mrs. Pitman seemed too stunned to say or do anything. But in spite of the life-threatening danger she faced, Heather had the feeling they weren't alone.

Then the train approached, its horn piercing the spring air and their thoughts.

"Mrs. Lewis, you're making a big mistake," Jenn implored. "Why would you want three counts of murder against you?"

The woman grinned evilly. "Okay, Pierce," she said to her accomplice. "Ready . . ."

Mrs. Pitman fainted, and Heather caught her arm to keep her from slipping to her death.

"Set . . . "

The train roared toward them!

"Go!" Mrs. Lewis's voice rose above the clamor of the train, and Heather braced herself for the deadly fall. *But it didn't come!* To their amazement Carl shouted, "Give it up!" and pointed his gun straight at Mrs. Lewis.

"Are you crazy?" she demanded.

Heather moved quickly, tripping Mrs. Lewis from behind. The weapon fell from her hand, and the woman lost her balance. She slid down the steep slope toward the train!

"Oh!" screamed Jenn. "I can't look!"

In a dizzying flurry of activity, Officer Florence Crane appeared from nowhere and made a daring lunge, barely snatching Mrs. Lewis from certain death. Her partner radioed for an ambulance that screeched around the back of the Music Fair in seconds.

Mrs. Pitman collapsed, and Jenn sank to the ground weak-kneed after the close brush with death. Emergency medical technicians helped them get back to the Music Fair's administrative offices. Although Heather felt a little shaky, too, her quick mind was already piecing together what had happened.

"Sorry to frighten you like that," Mrs. Lewis's partner apologized. He shook Heather's hand. "I'm actually Sergeant Carl Wechsler. Steven Ramsey had me come after that model got food poisoned."

"Thank God he did!" Heather exclaimed. "Then it was you who kidnapped Jenn and hit me on the head?"

"You're right about Jenn, but I didn't hit you. Mrs. Lewis did that before I could stop her." He faced the redhead. "We let your parents know you were safe." Then he grinned. "You were very courageous."

Jenn blushed as Heather tapped her on the shoulder. A group of people, including their parents, Brian, and Joe, rushed toward them and soon had the girls in happy, tearful embraces. Heather even got weepy when Ashley and Mrs. Pitman were reunited.

Yet not everyone was happy. Just down the hall Courtney watched the police take her mother away in handcuffs.

"Why, Mother?" she cried softly.

"I missed my chance years ago," she muttered. "I wasn't going to let anyone stand in your way."

Then Officer Straiter took her out the door to a waiting police car. Courtney walked away sadly. Heather would later learn she had dropped out of the competition.

Ashley came over and hugged both Heather and Jenn. "Thank you so much," she gushed. "You were wonderful!"

"Do you really think it's okay now?" Mrs. Pitman asked nervously.

The Reeds and McLaughlins seemed anxious too, thinking the mystery might not be completely solved.

"The danger has definitely passed," Chloé St. Johns reassured them as she approached the group.

"How do you know?" asked Mrs. Reed.

"Because the police also arrested Jean-Paul," she explained. "He can hurt no one else now."

"How did it happen?" Heather asked.

"After talking with you last night, the police watched him closely," Chloé began. "A couple of hours ago I was in the empty dressing area looking for Joan Winchell when Jean-Paul came in."

"Did he see you?" Heather's hazel eyes sparkled.

"No," she answered. "I hid."

"What did he do?"

"He put a note on Courtney Lewis's dressing table. I rushed to it when he left. It was addressed to the girl's mother. The handwriting caught my eye. Heather had told me about a threatening note written with a thick script. Mrs. Lewis's name was written in the same fashion. So I took it to a police officer."

"And?" Heather coaxed.

"It told Mrs. Lewis he would be leaving the country. He did not want any more of her scheme." Chloé got a twinkle in her eyes. "The police officer and I saw him sneak out of the Music Fair, but we caught up with him before he could get away. He said he wasn't feeling well." She paused. "Most likely he is not—Jean-Paul is now in police custody."

"Nice work!" the others praised her.

"So, I do believe the contest can now go on in a happy way," she concluded.

"I'm still wondering what happened with that falling stage light?" Heather mused. She had figured everything out except that.

"Jean-Paul got the boy who knocked you and Jenn down and slashed my tires to do that."

"And his connection with Mrs. Lewis?"

"She 'persuaded' him to promote Courtney. It seems that Mrs. Lewis found out Jean-Paul's secret about the stolen designs and was blackmailing him," Chloé explained. "But Jean-Paul could not go along with murder plans. That was Mrs. Lewis's idea, and that is why he tried to leave, according to the note I found."

Mrs. Pitman shook her head. "Oh, dear! Here comes the press, and just look at me!" She tried desperately to fix her hair and smooth her soiled clothes.

Everyone laughed—even Ashley. "Mother, you're practically a hero! Forget how you look for one second!"

The contest went on as scheduled, and a capacity crowd filled the Music Fair. Newspeople from around the country reported on the mystery and eagerly anticipated who would walk away with the huge prize.

"Before announcing the winners," Nathan Drake said, "we have a check from Pep Shampoo for the person who helped save lives and the American Model of the Year Contest—Miss Heather Reed!"

Heather, who'd been standing in the orchestra pit with the photographers, couldn't believe it. She made her way up on the circular stage. "Thank you," she said. "I'd like to share this with my friend, Jenn McLaughlin."

Nathan motioned for Jenn to take the stage as well, and the teenagers hugged each other happily. Then Heather and Jenn went back to their places.

"And now for the time we've all anticipated," the emcee declared, still full of his own importance. "The judges are deeply impressed with the way each contestant handled herself during the week. So is Pep Shampoo, which will give each runner-up the opportunity to do an ad for them." After the applause died down, he took an envelope from Chloé St. Johns. "And the winner is—Kirsten Neff!"

Kirsten came forward escorted by a beaming Brian. She smiled happily as she accepted a bouquet of roses, kisses from Marci Bentley and Luke Granger, and a check for $25,000 from Steven Ramsey. Then she glided up and down the runway, waving to the live audience in the Music Fair and to the millions watching on TV.

Afterward at a reception, Heather told Chloé St. Johns, "Kirsten's quite a winner."

"And you're quite a detective!" the fashion editor smiled.

"Thanks," Heather blushed. "I just hope another mystery comes along soon. I already miss the action!"

Jenn grumbled. "Not me! All I want to do is sleep for a week!"